# Cold As Ice

## Tiffany Casper

### As If...
#### Book 1

Copyright © Tiffany Casper 2022

All rights reserved. No part of this publication may be reproduced, distributed, or transmitted in any form or by any means, including photocopying, recording, or other electronic or mechanical methods, without the prior written permission of the publisher, except in the case of brief quotations embodied in critical reviews and certain other noncommercial uses permitted by copyright law. Any references to historical events, real people, or real places are used fictitiously. Names, characters, and places are products of the author's imagination.

## Dedication

Some authors always say that the hardest part about writing a book is this part. Well thankfully, so far, I haven't had that problem... knock on wood.

For me, the hardest part is choosing which character would be best to start the story lol.

## Acknowledgements

Editor - Shelby Limon

My Beta team, y'all rock!

My ARC team, y'all are awesome sauce!

## Blurb:

Club girls never get their happily ever after.

It was a known fact.

However, for the men of Zagan MC, they didn't give a damn.

Only they didn't realize the battle that they would need to win.

Their hearts.

Because a girl didn't wake up and declare she was going to be a Club Girl.

This is Gabriella & Pipe's story.

## Song

Iris – The Goo Goo Dolls

## Zagan MC

Asher – President

Whit – Vice President

Priest – Enforcer

Rome – SGT at Arms

Pipe – Secretary

Trigger – Treasurer

Charlie – Teck Guru

Irish – Road Captain

Coal – Icer

**Table Of Contents**

Prologue
Chapter 1
Chapter 2
Chapter 3
Chapter 4
Chapter 5
Chapter 6
Chapter 7
Chapter 8
Chapter 9
Chapter 10
Chapter 11
Chapter 12
Epilogue
Thank You Note
Other Works
Connect With Me

# Prologue
## Pipe

What would it be like to be with a woman that didn't always say they loved you?

But showed you.

How would it feel to never hear the words *I need you*, but that they could convey that with one look?

Would it matter to her that I didn't bring in six figures a year?

Did she really care about my socks never matching because I tossed them wherever they landed?

Or did she just shake her head and pick them up on her way to the laundry room? Or… did she just grab them and trash them?

Did she really care about my needs?

So much that she left dinner in the oven for me so it could keep warm?

Did she keep my favorite beer stocked?

Did she toss a towel in the dryer for me to use after a shower so I could be comfortable?

Would she recognize when I've had a bad day, walk up behind me, wrap her arms around me, and just be there for me?

How would it feel to finally have all of that?

"Pipe. Are you ready?" I cringed when my wife asked me that.

No, I wasn't ready. I didn't think I would ever be ready to be seen with her out in public again, not after the last time.

The last time? We were getting groceries. I had one cart for the things I wanted, and she had another cart for the things she wanted. Apparently, because they didn't have her favorite brand of chips that cost eight dollars a freaking bag, she threw a tantrum right there in the middle of the store. And then I had to hear about going to that certain store because I was tired from a run helping another club and didn't want to travel over an hour to another store that she preferred. All because it catered to the rich. And it always had her favorite chips in stock.

And if I were being honest, I never touched her out in public either. Not just because of the tantrums she threw but the fact that I wanted to be associated with her as little as possible.

But alas, I was young and dumb and didn't understand that women were spiteful and sneaky as hell when I asked her to marry me seventeen long-ass years ago.

"Yeah," I grumbled out as I got up off the couch, holding in the wince that wanted to burst forth, and walked to where my kutte was hanging beside the door.

Today, I was having the nomad patch on my kutte removed, and I was having Mississippi put on the bottom rocker where it rightfully belongs.

Shrugging the kutte on my shoulders, I grimaced as I pulled my arms up and felt the pull of my ribs. Four weeks later and they still hurt like a motherfucker.

"Hurry up, Pipe. We should have been there half an hour ago." She snapped as she walked to the door, still inserting an earring in her ear. Of fucking course.

Did she help me with my kutte? Fuck no.

Were we not late because she had to apply half of her makeup stock on her face? Again, apparently fucking not.

I held that shit in. It wouldn't do any good to remind her that we were late because of her.

It would have been like talking to a brick fucking wall.

Besides, I never felt the need to tell her she didn't need to wear that war paint.

In all honesty, she fucking needed it.

I know what you're thinking…

What kind of man did that make me when I say that my wife looks better with a shit ton of makeup on?

It was true.

She didn't resemble the woman I had fallen for all those years ago. Or what I thought fallen had meant at the time.

But not anymore.

Not with the Botox, the lip fillers, and the nose job she just had to have. Not to mention the boob job and implants in her ass. Yes, I shit you not. Implants in her ass.

Now don't get me wrong, I was all for women improving their bodies if it made them happy. But did any of that turn me on? Hell fucking no. It was fake. Pure and simple.

Were there any women out there that were so comfortable in their own skin that they didn't mess with what they were given by their parents?

If I ever found a woman that was, I would kneel before her feet.

Little did I know, I would be eating my words in just a few short minutes.

After I climbed on my bike, and she climbed into her car that her daddy paid for because I refused to buy her something that flashy, we headed to the clubhouse.

And let me make this perfectly clear, she is the one that never wanted to ride on the back of my bike, not the other way around. And after the first year of being together, and practically asking her every day to go for a ride with me, I quit asking.

When we pulled into the clubhouse, I saw the confused look on her face through her car window when I didn't back my bike into the long line of them in front of the clubhouse. Rather, I pulled into a random spot and shut her down.

I knew what was coming the moment she turned off her ignition, opened the door, and climbed out, "Why didn't you pull over there? You're not a nomad anymore."

"Because the vote is today. I don't have the right to park with them yet, considering I'm still technically a nomad." I said through gritted teeth. Seventeen years with me, and she still didn't know or really care how shit worked. She didn't understand anything that was outside of her little small-minded circle.

She huffed, then grabbed a bag that I again wouldn't pay for because that bag alone could have covered groceries for six months, and closed her door with her fucking hip. Jesus H Christ. She loved the car so much, gushed when she got it, and risked putting a dent in it with the force she used? Fucking typical of Rebecca Edwards Childers.

I was walking to the front door of the clubhouse when something out of the corner of my eye caught my attention.

Unknowingly, I stopped and felt Rebecca walk into my back as I turned my head to see what was going on. I heard her let out an oomph and then a snarl at the fact that she touched me at all.

Yeah, in case you missed that, we slept in separate beds too.

Now, let me tell you something else, not once have I ever cheated.

Have I thought about it?

Fuck yeah, I have.

I'm a red-blooded male. Sex is fucking important. That release, sliding into a woman's tight heat and rocking both of our worlds. It's something else.

As for the vision in front of me? Fucking hell. I would have cheated a long ass time ago to have that.

And then like a flash into the future or some shit, I saw the woman that was sitting in that truck bed, her dark hair fanned out over my pillow, her body rubbing deliciously under mine. Her moans. Her breaths. The way she sounded when she came. The way her eyes shined as she came while staring into my own. Seeing her swollen with my child in her belly. The whole nine yards.

Just like that, I was hard as a fucking rock.

And then I felt like a total creeper and a fucking pervert. Because I was thirty-five years old, and she couldn't be no more than twenty-four at most. Not to mention I haven't seen her before, so I had no clue if she was an ole' lady either.

With just the top half of her body visible, I knew... I knew that everything about that woman was natural. If she were standing before me, you best believe I would've dropped to my knees in front of her.

But... just then seeing the woman that climbed down from the truck bed and got to her knees because she saw a little girl that was running fall down?

Any woman that can stop what they are doing and help a child, that was a good woman.

What shocked the hell out of me was that there were at least five people in the back of that truck bed, and at least fifty people surrounding it.

And no one else stopped what they were doing to check on her.

Without knowing it, my feet moved in their direction.

And when I heard, "Now, smile that big toothy grin that is going to make all the boys fall at their feet. Then I want you to remember something, something important. It's okay to cry. What's not okay is to think you aren't beautiful when you do. That crying makes you weak because it doesn't. And I'll tell you something I want you to hold onto for the rest of your life, okay?" She waited for the little girl with blonde hair in pigtails to nod as she wiped the back of her hand across her nose, and then the mystery woman continued, "When you get married, that person is going to feel as though they were the luckiest person on the planet, and if they don't tear up when they lay eyes on you for the first time in your elegant princess dress, I want you to turn around throw up the peace sign then march your cute little bootie back up that aisle and go on your honeymoon by yourself."

"Powerful words, Gabby," I heard a man say as he walked up to them and then something strange happened inside of me.

When he ran his hand along the back of her neck... fucking hell, I wanted to march over there, rip the fucker's arm from his body and then beat him with it.

It was Buster. The fucker was married or at least he had been. Why the fuck was he touching her like that?

Was she his wife?

I remembered his wife, and I don't remember her looking like this.

"Pipe, it's hot. Can we go inside now?" Upon hearing her voice, I completely forgot that Rebecca was standing there.

But did I move from my spot?

Hell no.

*Turn your head my way, darlin'. I wanna see those eyes.*

Sadly, I almost pouted when she didn't look my way, but rather she pulled away from Buster's touch, tapped the little girl on the nose, then climbed back inside the back of the truck as I watched water slosh a little over the side in that black string bikini I wanted to remove from her body with my teeth.

I didn't pout.

No, I fucking smiled when she had moved from Buster's touch, and it took everything in me to not laugh outright when Buster frowned and then shot her a glare.

That right there did something to my heart.

It fucking cracked the smallest of amounts.

And why?

I have no motherfucking clue.

Just who was this woman? Never did I ever imagine I would find someone that could take all my attention off what I was doing. Hell, even my wife hadn't been able to do that.

Without a word to my wife… I'm married. I'm married. I'm married. I turned back and stalked into the clubhouse, and no I didn't open the door so she could go in first.

I know that made me a dick.

But I had a reason to be one.

And I wasn't going to allow all the shit that has happened over the past thirty-five years of my life to take away this feeling.

This feeling of, for the first time in my life, seeing someone that I honestly wanted to come home to everyday.

Someone I wanted to wrap my arms around and smile because she had chosen me to be her man.

Someone who, with one look in my direction, could make me feel like I was finally home.

A feeling I have never experienced before.

And one that would happen just after church.

## Chapter 1
### Gabby – Earlier That Morning

"Today is going to be a great day," Lizette told me as she flipped pancakes while I made the tenth omelet this morning.

She was right, too. Today was going to be a great day.

Here in a little while, Asher promised the women we could get a giant tarp and put it in the back of the truck and fill it full of water so we could get cool.

After that, we were having a barbeque with burgers and hot dogs because they had some allied clubs coming in for the weekend as well as Wrath MC was coming to visit. Not to mention, they were patching in two prospects and the rumor around the clubhouse was that they had a man that had gone nomad for reasons none of us girls know, and he was coming back today to get his patch. Hopefully.

The other club girls would be open for whatever, but not me. I was off today from working because I was babysitting the little ones during the party with Asher's daughter, Stella. Which I was grateful for. One of the prospects was disgusting, and on top of that, with the other men coming in, Asher had given the order that the club girls would be with any of the men.

Not to mention, if their ole' ladies couldn't come with them, I had no way to tell if the men were claimed or not because some of them didn't wear wedding bands.

Just as I plated the tenth omelet, I had two more to go when Whit walked up behind me and caged me in with the stove. "Hey doll, got a minute you can spare for me?" Whit asked as he ran his nose along the column of my neck. I knew what he was asking for.

"You got it, big man, soon as I finish the dishes," I told him and got a wink in response.

I liked Whit. He was a decent guy. He was also the Vice President of Zagan MC.

Just as I finished the last two omelets and ate my own food, Lizette and I knocked out the dishes when Sutton came walking into the kitchen.

She headed for the fridge to get her yogurt and then to the pantry to grab her granola.

Seeing the hickeys on her neck, I snorted, "You get branded last night?"

I asked her and saw a blush form on her cheeks.

Just then, Irish walked into the kitchen, tagging the last plate with the last omelet on it.

Sutton watched him walk to a table, sit, and chow down. All the while pretending she was eating her own food, but one glance at her and you knew she was sitting in that position so she could keep an eye on him from the corner of her eye.

When he was finished, he stood up, brought me the plate with a wink then walked out.

All the while, Sutton followed his movements with longing in her eyes while she ate her yogurt and granola.

And when I noticed that he hadn't spared her a backward glance, I saw her shoulders drop.

Grabbing a hand towel, I dried my hands after I washed his plate and fork, then I walked over to Sutton and said, "Honey, as far as I know, he hasn't slept with any of the other club girls."

She looked up at me with a tear trailing down the corner of her eye and smiled weakly. "I know. Pres is getting pretty pissed off at him, I do know that. He claims I'm his, but he won't do anything about it either. He warns all the brothers that try to come onto me, too."

"He doesn't want you but doesn't want anyone else to have you?" I was a blunt person. I didn't see the need to sugarcoat anything.

She nodded solemnly. "Maybe it's time to move on. We've been doing this dance for over a year now."

"You going to try to be with one of the other brothers tonight?" I asked her, knowing that was the direction she was more than likely going in. It wasn't fair to her that Irish was stringing her along like he was.

"I'm thinking about it. But I just… I don't want whoever it is to get hurt. You saw what happened the last time a brother from another chapter grabbed me around the waist while we were dancing." She visibly shuttered, obviously remembering in grave detail what had happened.

The guy that she had been dancing with had wrapped his hand around her back to pull her in closer, and where his hand had landed? It was right at the top of her ass. It really was nothing, but it wasn't to Irish.

He had stormed over there, grabbed the man's hand, and wrenched his arm back too far. We all heard a pop when he dislocated the guy's shoulder.

As if that wasn't enough, Irish had grabbed Sutton, pulled her behind him, and then while he still held onto the guy's arm, he maneuvered him to the ground, roughly, then with one of his steel toe boots he slammed it down hard into his side.

And that, my friend, was how that other guy suffered four broken ribs, a punctured lung, and a dislocated shoulder, not to mention torn tendons.

"You can always talk to Asher," I told her.

"I could, but after what happened with Hallie this morning, I don't want to stir up any more drama."

What was on the tip of my tongue was to tell her that one of the club women that came with the other clubs was going to make a beeline for Irish.

Every time she came here, she was in his bed. And when she left, he was back in Sutton's.

I hated it for Sutton. She didn't deserve to be treated that way, but we were club girls. We had made the choice.

"I have to watch the kids tonight, and knowing Stella, she will shoo me out of the room so I can enjoy the party. I'll run interference if you want me to."

"You're awesome, girl. I think that would be great." Smiling, I nodded, then winked at her and walked out of the kitchen to the main part of the clubhouse.

Seeing Whit sitting there at one of the tables, I walked over to him, and of course, added sway in my hips.

He saw me coming, his eyes running up and down my body, all the while licking his lips.

When I made it to him, I walked around him, running the tips of my fingers up his strong arm and then around the back of his neck. Leaning forward while my breast rubbed his kutte, I whispered in his ear, "You ready, handsome?"

He stood up then, twirled, wrapped an arm around my waist, and then hauled me up, all the while smashing his mouth with mine.

Catcalls from the men serenaded us as he led me down the hall and to the right where our rooms were.

Walking into my room, our mouths separated, he let go of my waist, and then he sat down on my bed. Knowing what he wanted, I walked over to plug my phone into my little Bluetooth speaker and started up one of my favorite songs, *A Little Wicked by Valerie Broussard*.

After I stripped my clothes off with tantalizing moves, I stood before Whit and by the time I had the last piece of clothing off, he was up and shredding out of his clothes.

Walking to the bedside table, I pulled open the drawer and grabbed an unopened box of condoms, and handed them to him. Asher had handed us all mini packs of condoms that were all unopened this morning. If the guy didn't have one, we were to hand them an unopened box so they would know that they were not tampered with.

"Darlin', you could've handed me one that was already opened. We all trust you."

I shrugged. "I tossed them already. Besides, y'all need the reassurance that the others won't do something that terrible."

He simply nodded, opened the box, pulled out a foil, opened it, and then slid the piece of latex over his cock.

His cock was already hard, and long, with a deep purple head.

Climbing on the bed, I got on my hands and knees and wiggled my ass for him.

Either my body had gotten used to the intrusion that almost always happened, or I had no hopes of ever getting wet enough for them to just slip inside.

\*\*\*

"Yes, honey, just like that," I said as Whit moved inside of me, thrusting and moaning.

Breathlessly, he asked, "You like that, baby?"

"Mmhmm, so good." I was lying through my freaking teeth.

He never got me off.

What I really wanted was for him to get done, get off me, let me shower and finish myself off. After that, I can get a juicy cheeseburger, then climb into the back of Asher's truck bed for an impromptu pool party. All in that order.

When I felt him pull out and slap my ass, I turned my head to look at him over my shoulder and smile. Thank fucking God.

After he tore off the condom, tied it, and tossed it in my wastebasket, he pulled on his clothes, pressed a kiss to my lips, and then he walked out of the room.

I all but raced to the shower, and there I brought my own damn self to orgasm, using the water to muffle the sounds of my release.

Standing in the shower, I allowed the hot water to run along my body, and then when it started to get cold, I turned off the water, grabbed my fluffy white towel, and dried myself off.

There's some truth to the saying that you are what your mother made you.

At least in my case, that was God's honest truth.

When you hear every day, "I don't know why you are trying so hard in school, you won't be going anywhere like me."

Oh, and my personal favorite, "You've got good looks from me, a body that men cry over, use it."

So, when around our small town, your own mother is known as a town tramp, they automatically loop you into that same category, never mind that you are still a virgin at the time.

And one day while I was waiting for my turn to get my toes done, I heard a woman named Lizette talking about all the things she was able to have because of our local MC. I walked over and talked to her.

And the rest, as they say, is history.

I've been a club girl for over a year now and thanks to Lizette, I finally found a place where I felt as if I truly belonged.

Not only did I have a roof over my head, food at the ready, hot men to look at all day, but I also made the calls.

The only two I ever made were that I didn't sleep with married men, and I didn't take it up the ass. Everything else was fair game.

I also got to say no when I was on the rag. Because believe me, there were some brothers that got off on that stuff, and it was just freaking weird.

However, there was something that I have never experienced. You know the feeling you get when you look at someone… someone that is fucking edible and delicious and just so mesmerizing that it does something to your body?

The one where you get wet and have to tighten your thighs to stay in control of your body?

The feeling erupts without them even having to touch you…

What I didn't know was even though I've never had this feeling, I would be getting it later in the day.

## Chapter 2
### Pipe

Once we entered the main room of the clubhouse, my eyes landed on Asher as he nodded, then he looked over to Whit and waved two fingers.

As soon as every brother was in the room we used for church, with our phones sitting in a box on a table right outside of the room, the doors were closed.

Was it bad that I had clocked the woman I had seen in the back of that truck bed walking through the main room and down a hall, but I couldn't tell you where my wife went? Probably.

As soon as Asher banged the gavel on the table that held the insignia for Zagan MC, a fire-breathing dragon with skulls littering the ground at his feet, everyone stopped talking.

I stood with my arms crossed against the back wall.

"Not only is one of our own coming home to stay and retake his bottom rocker, but we also have two prospects that we need to vote on whether they have what it takes to become a brother."

Everyone nodded and then Asher spoke to me, "Pipe, known you for a lot of years. Only a few of us know why you left, so you need to explain before we take it to a vote."

I nodded, then took in a deep breath and started, "Most of you know I'm married. No. I didn't make her my ole' lady. At first, she wanted it, but she never wanted to come to club parties when I prospected, and she never wanted to ride on the back of my bike. Her father is from the right side of the tracks, and I was from the wrong side. I fell in love with her instantly. Well, what I thought love was, but I was a goddamned fool. She only married me to piss her father off because he wouldn't buy her the car she wanted. She got it anyway. And when she tried to divorce me, her father told her she couldn't. That it has never happened in their family, and she wasn't going to be the one to start it because she threw a temper tantrum.

Anyway, her father is a bigwig. We're talking running for the senate and shit. So, when he let us know that he wanted all of us with him on his campaign trail, I fucking tried. I tried to be a good husband despite the shit she threw at me. I had made vows, and I fully intended to carry them out. That was why I went nomad. Without the kutte, and when she threw her temper tantrums in restaurants and crap, I had to handle business myself. Five on one, I could handle, but not ten on one. That was the first time I really grew to resent her. I'm talking about we don't sleep in the same bed, or even in the same room, and we haven't in over ten years. I've also been faithful, where she has not.

    I know what you're thinking. Why have I stuck it out this long, and not divorced her ass, and why am I just now coming back to my brothers? I got my ass handed to me. She slept with an underboss. One who was married to the daughter of the capo and if it wasn't for her, he wouldn't be an underboss. So, she put the call to her family to have my wife taken out, but me being me, being loyal as fuck to her for fuck-all I don't know why I defended her when ten men stormed into our house three months ago. I just got done with physical therapy and I will always carry a limp. The only reason she and I are still breathing was because of my loyalty to her.

Now, why am I back here finally? Because I have finally had enough. I broke and did something I vowed I would never do. When she didn't come to the hospital while I was in surgery to fix the mess they had created. When she didn't come to my physical therapy appointments, I got home and found her in her bed with two other men. I didn't do a damn thing to them, but I did backhand my wife. Now, to the question of why I am still married to the she-bitch from hell, her father has a video. When I was jumped by five men, I killed all five of them. If that video ever surfaces, I'm looking at twenty years to life in a maximum-security prison. Doesn't matter that it was self-defense in my eyes. They had started to retreat, you can see it in the video, only I didn't let them walk out of that alley alive. If I don't stay married to his daughter, that video will be released."

I swallowed then; I needed a drink.

Luckily, Whit, the VP, stood up, opened the door, and called for beers.

And to my amazement, the woman that had my undivided attention stepped into the doorway to the room with a tray of beers. She kept her head down, and only when the tray was out of her hands, she grabbed the handle and closed the doors.

I wasn't angry after retelling everything, no I was angry that I still didn't know the color of her eyes.

Whit handed me a beer as he then passed the others out, and as soon as I had the top opened, I took a long drink, then swallowed.

"Okay, the floor is open," Asher said as Charlie raised his hand and when Asher nodded, Charlie looked at me.

"Where is the video at?" Charlie asked.

"It's on a flash drive in his wall safe in his house. He never told me if they have more than one copy."

Charlie nodded, then he opened his laptop and started typing.

While he did that Irish looked at me and said, "Admire trying to make it work. Never hit a woman, don't intend to start. But no one, and I mean no one, would blame you for what you did."

I nodded in thanks and took another pull from my beer.

That was when Charlie spoke, "I found the original video on his server, and it looks like he made one copy. Do you know how he got the video?"

I snarled then, "My fucking wife."

Around the room, the men cursed and shook their heads. "Her excuse was that it turned her on, which is a bunch of shit."

Charlie was typing away on his laptop, and then asked, "What's your wife's number?" I rattled it off and then waited.

A few minutes passed as he frowned, hit one key, and then fucking smiled. "The video is gone from her phone. And the video is gone from the server. We need to plan and get the flash drive from his place."

Everything in my body relaxed at hearing I had someone backing me. If they voted me back into the club, I would have all of them at my back again. Oh, what a feeling that was.

I watched as Asher took in the room and the men were gathered around the table as he asked, "Okay, we ready to vote?"

All the men nodded but it was Rome who spoke up, "Even if you didn't have a reason to come back home you just wanted to, my vote still would have been yes. Appreciate you handling that shit you did while you were nomad." I nodded at him.

I had tracked down the men and ended them. Ones that their father had allowed to gang-rape Rome's sister, all to pay a debt of ten grand. Ten fucking grand.

"All in favor of Pipe returning to the club, raise your hand," Asher called out, and damn if every man in the club raised their hands.

He nodded, then slammed the gavel. "Welcome back home, brother. Our paperwork is a mess, get on that immediately. Pipe is our Secretary." I nodded gratefully and then took the chair beside Coal.

After I had my ass in my seat, Asher said, "Now we need to vote on the two prospects. The vote has to be unanimous. The first is for Alec. We all know he has put in his time, never once disrespected us, helps out with whatever is asked of him, and he does shit without being told to do so. All in favor of Alec?"

Every man's hand in the room went up. I had gotten the intel from my brothers about the two prospects, and I knew all I needed to know about them. And I knew a little bit more about one of them that I didn't like. Not one God damned bit.

Asher nodded, then slammed the gavel on the table.

"Now we need to vote for Tanner. He's had his issues, same as some of us, but he's been a good prospect. He's always there when you need him. All in favor, raise your hands."

Every man's hand went up in the air but four of them, mine, Asher's, Charlie's, and Irish's.

Asher nodded then said, "Now since the vote isn't unanimous, we need to know why the four are saying no. Charlie, you go first."

Charlie nodded, then spoke, "He needs to account for the weekly payments of five grand that have been hitting his account over the past two months, and he needs to explain why I can't trace them."

Asher nodded, "That's my reason too. I think he's working with the feds. He doesn't know that Charlie can hack into everything. Pipe, your turn."

"We don't allow drugs in the club; sure, we allow pot and that's it. Saw him making deals, handing over cash, and taking something from a guy. Gave the guy a beat down and found out it was crank. That happened three days ago. I called Asher about it, and he told me that because we were voting to save it for this meeting, so you could all be made aware of it."

Asher nodded, then he looked at Irish, "I already got a feeling what you're going to say, and I am going to say you need to claim that girl as your ole' lady and stop this shit with her, but let's hear it."

"He plans to make Sutton his ole' lady when he gets his patch. He also plans to sleep around on her. He already told me what his road name is, already went too far with that shit since we are the ones that hand out road names. It's fucking Lucky."

"Anyone else have anything to add?" Asher asked as he looked around the room.

When nobody spoke, he nodded. "With the vote not being unanimous, Tanner will not be getting his patch and he will be escorted off the property. Priest, you make sure that fucker goes."

All Priest did was nod.

"Irish, you need to claim that girl and be done with it," Asher told him with a stern glower.

And what did Irish do? He fucking shrugged.

I didn't know who Sutton was.

Didn't really care.

As long as he wasn't after the woman that Buster had called Gabby. Fuck, please don't let her be his ole' lady.

Asher looked at Rome and said, "Bring them in here."

Rome stood, then opened the door and hollered for the two prospects.

Knowing what I know now about the two of them, I was glad the vote went the way it did.

Alec walked in here with sweat beading along his brow and went to stand where I had.

But Tanner, well, he walked in all cocky-like and looked around the table and had the balls to ask, "Where is my chair at?"

You could've heard a pin drop when Coal spoke, low and menacing, "Wish I hadn't thrown my hand up for him now."

And everyone took notice of his words. Coal *only* spoke when something really important mattered to him. It was also known that the one person he spoke to often was Adeline, one of the club girls. I was told that by Asher when he gave me the rundown on the club a few months ago when I told him I was planning on coming back.

Asher's voice dropped low and menacing when he said, "You little shit. You haven't even heard the vote, so it means you're not a brother yet. Take your goddamn ass over to that wall and stand beside Alec. And if you so much as to say a word, I'll cut you from your ass to your fucking elbow."

Thankfully, Tanner listened and did as he was told. And when I saw that eye roll, I pulled my gun from the inside of my kutte and cocked it back, then I pointed it at his head, "You ever disrespect our Pres. again and I won't hesitate to pull this trigger. Fucking understood?"

Asher raised a brow at me, and I said, "Fucker rolled his goddamn eyes."

"Let me kill him. Now." Priest said as he pulled out a knife and started to roll the blade between his fingertips.

Asher shook his head with a ghost of a smile on his face. "Alec, step forward."

Alec did so and then Asher looked at him, and I had to give the kid credit. He stood there, chin raised, shoulders back, ready to hear his fate with everything he was.

"Welcome to Zagan MC. Your road name is fitting, and you are now known as Pagan." Asher nodded at Whit who stood up, walked over to the filing cabinet, and pulled out our bottom rocker, along with one for me, and then a one percent patch as well as the patch that held his road name on it already stitched.

He handed the Mississippi rocker to me, and then the two to Pagan along with his road name patch. Whit gestured to one of the chairs in the corner. "Take your place across from Pipe."

Pagan nodded and then did as he was instructed.

We waited for him to settle in his seat.

"Tanner, you've done everything asked of you, and you know that when we vote for a prospect to become a brother, the vote has to be unanimous. Unlike the vote for Pagan, which was unanimous, yours wasn't. We talked about why some of the brothers don't trust you, and we all agree. You will not be getting your patch. Priest, please ensure that he gets all of his shit and is off club property immediately."

And then the dumb fuck spoke. "What? What have I done to make them not trust me?"

Asher laughed dangerously, "You want to tell us why you were spotted buying crank? Wanna tell us where the five grand every week for the past two months that's been hitting your account is from and for what? Wanna tell us why you already have a road name when we haven't given you one yet? And wanna tell us why you plan to make a club girl an ole' lady when we all know she has eyes for Irish?"

His eyes had widened when he found out we knew about that money.

Something in my gut was telling me I needed to check for something. I locked eyes with Rome, and he nodded, sensing the same thing I was.

We both stood and then jumped on him. Rome held his arms back while I raised his shirt, and low and behold, there was a wire taped to his chest.

"Son of a bitch." Was murmured by every club member.

"We can't kill the bastard," Asher grumbled. "Fuck it, Priest, get this pig off our property. Pipe, you, and Coal go through his room, go through every fucking thing and if you don't find anything, then box his shit and toss it over the fucking gate." The gavel was slammed down as Priest hauled Tanner out of the room while he was shouting at us and cursing us every name under the sun.

We all followed them out as everyone in the main room stopped what they were doing to take the scene in.

My eyes trailed through the room, looking for her. And when my eyes landed on her, fucking hell. She was fucking stunning.

She was still wearing that coverup over her bikini, and I wanted to throw her over my shoulder, take her far, far away where there were no prying eyes to see her smooth tanned skin.

But it wasn't what she had on that had me thinking she was stunning.

No, it was the way she smiled down at that same little girl that belonged to Gravel, the same one that had fallen down.

I turned and followed Coal down the hallway, but stopped and looked back into the room, just now realizing that when I walked out of church, my eyes hadn't even looked for Rebecca. She hadn't even been on my mind. But now, my eyes scanned it for my wife. Not seeing her, I stopped a club girl that was walking past me into the kitchen and asked, "The woman, the one with the sleek hair, fake as fuck rich ass, you know where she went?"

She nodded. "Yeah, she spoke to Stella after her phone rang and said she had to go because of a headache."

I nodded my thanks, then followed Coal to the room the prospects used and went through Tanner's room.

Sure enough, there were journals and recordings of shit he shouldn't have.

# Chapter 3
## Gabby

After Priest had hauled one of the prospects out of the clubhouse, the one named Tanner, I smiled at Alec, who walked over to me holding onto his kutte and his new patches. When he asked me to help him, I nodded.

"Follow me to my room. I've got my sewing kit in there."

After I had the prospect one off, and then his three new patches on the kutte, I held it up and helped him put it on.

Seeing the patch, I smiled, "Pagan. I like it."

He nodded, then asked, "Wanna be my congratulations present?"

I tossed my head back and laughed. "Not going to waste any time, are you?"

He shook his head then bit his lip. I tapped his bottom lip then shook my head and told him, "I'm off the rest of the afternoon, and after the cookout I'm watching the kids."

He nodded then and strode for the doorway while I put everything away, but he stopped and said, "You're something else, Gabby. Admire you, darlin'."

I smiled and nodded.

After everything was put away, I walked out of my room. Thankfully, my bikini had time to dry, and I still had on my cover-up.

I walked through the main room of the clubhouse and out to the back courtyard where Adeline, Lizette, and Sutton were sitting still in their bikinis while holding glasses of margaritas.

When Sutton saw me, she smiled and grabbed the other margarita that was resting on the arm of my chair and waved me over.

Taking off my cover-up, I settled into the lounger and took a grateful sip of the delicious goodness.

That was when the gabbing between women started, "I swear, there is one man I want. Well, make that three of them." Lizette said.

Settling into my lounge chair fully, I asked, "Who?"

"Asher, Rome, and Priest. Jesus Christ." Lizette said, and I knew she said the other two names to hide how she was feeling about Rome.

I kept it to myself that I had Asher. God, that man. But I haven't had him in a year. Not since I started seeing the way he looked at his daughter's best friend. And as far as I know, he hasn't been with anyone else. That much was true. Even more so when the other girls each nodded their heads in understanding.

"Priest. He doesn't trust easily. Not after what his ex-wife did to him."

We all knew about that, too. Priest had been head over heels for that woman. Loved her like no other. Married her, even made her his ole' lady, and everyone knew he was trying to get her pregnant.

See, when every girl joins, she gets a condensed light version of the member's past, so we know what to avoid with them.

And for Priest, that was mentioning anything about his ex-wife. Because the moment one said her name, he turned into a completely different person.

I've had to witness it one time when Hallie, the club girl that had been kicked out on her ass this morning, asked him about her.

He had torn apart the entire main room of the clubhouse. I'm talking breaking tables and chairs, scattering the food that was on the bar to the floor, punching holes in the walls. It wasn't pretty.

It wasn't pretty in the least but that had also taken place during Stella's sweet sixteen bash. If it had been for any other reason than Hallie mentioning that woman's name, Asher would have beaten the dog shit out of Priest. And we all knew Asher may be older, but he could take any man in the clubhouse out and down without even breaking a sweat.

But I digress… anyway, why mentioning her name turns Priest into a different person is because he had gotten her pregnant. Three times in the time they were married, and without saying a word to him, she had abortions for every single one.

What made it a lot worse was that five years ago, when the club had been attacked, Priest had taken a bullet just at his bottom rib when he dove in front of Asher to save him.

So that caused the bullet to ricochet inside of his body and exit out of his thigh. The doc at the clubhouse patched him up and everything was thought to be okay because nothing appeared to be alarming. He was lucky in that regard.

But that hadn't been the case, far freaking from it.

He was bruised from slamming into the floor, and he had thought that he had hit his balls on something going down. That wasn't the case.

After a week of the pain getting worse and worse, he went to the hospital where he learned that the bullet had indeed hit something monumental. It had severed the sperm duct that led to his balls.

Sadly, that had made him infertile. Had his wife not done what she had, he would've had the kids he wanted desperately.

I was brought back to the here and now when Lizette squirmed in her chair, my eyes scanned to the area she was looking at. I saw the reason for it. Rome.

Rome has been with the club about ten years after it started and considering Asher started the club when he was eighteen and he is now forty-five. That's a lot of years.

"But Rome… I just can't understand that man. One moment he's hot, then one moment he's cold."

Just as she said that, Rome walked by us with Coal at his side. I held my breath when Coal knelt beside Adeline's chair and whispered in her ear.

She was the only one that he spoke to besides his brothers. For everyone else, he would either give us a chin lift or a growl. And that was it.

And then, as I saw her cheeks blush, he stood and continued walking into the clubhouse.

"What was that all about?" Sutton asked her as she wiggled her eyebrows.

"He umm… well… he told me that my place tonight was on his lap, and at his side, no matter what." The rest of what we are sure he told her was left unsaid.

Basically, *you're mine tonight.*

Smiling at her, I thought about Rome. Ever since he made that trip to the Wrath MC, Tennessee chapter, he has been different.

"Did something happen out there?" I asked them, knowing they would know what I was talking about.

"We don't know. But I can tell you that I may have eavesdropped on a conversation that could probably land me in a heap of trouble. Oh, I can't keep it in. Something about one of their daughters had treated him in a way he's never felt before and he told Charlie to run her biological mother through the system. He wanted everything Charlie could find on her." Lizette said as her eyes trailed after Rome, who had disappeared into the clubhouse.

Lizette had only hidden her want with her statement from earlier. Everyone knows that she has stars in her eyes when she looks at Rome. Not like the ones Adeline has for Coal. And Sutton for Irish. She is simply infatuated with the man.

Just as I was about to take another sip of my margarita, Stella ran out of the clubhouse and over to me, rushing out, "Hey Gabby, can you help me in the kitchen?"

I nodded, then stood up, grabbed my cover-up, and pulled it over my body. The last thing I did was grab my glass.

Following Stella into the clubhouse, I had my head down, buttoning up my coverup one-handed, when I ran smack dab into the hardest chest known to man.

"Oomph," I said, and luckily my glass didn't spill all the way over the rim.

"Oh my gosh, Pipe, I am so sorry. Gabby wasn't watching where she was going." Stella hurriedly explained about me running into the man.

Looking up and then up and then up, the moment my eyes locked with his, there was that feeling. The one that settled deep in your marrow. The one that traveled down to your lady bits and ignited a fire inside of you, unlike anything you have ever felt before.

When my eyes locked with his, I saw his eyes widen.

And before I could ask about that, Stella grabbed my arm and pulled me around the man, I hadn't even understood what she had called him, and dragged me through the main room of the clubhouse and then into the kitchen.

"Jesus fucking Christ. Who was that?" I panted as I asked Stella as I followed her into the kitchen to help get dinner started.

It wasn't my night to cook, but the girl whose responsibility it was for tonight wasn't here to do it because she had been kicked out of the MC and banned for life.

How did that happen?

Simple, she broke one of their five rules.

Rule One: No talking about what happens on club property. Ever.

Rule Two: No trying to trap the brothers.

Rule Three: No sleeping with men who are not a part of the MC.

Rule Three, Subsection A: You could but you must have approval from Asher.

Rule Four: You can't say no to a brother.

Rule Five: You never disrespect a brother.

They really were simple.

But guess which rule Hallie broke?

Yep. Rule Two.

See, there are two types of club girls. Well, they are really called kutte chasers. The ones who think that spreading their legs for every man in the MC in the hopes that one of them will fall in love with her pussy so much that he will make her an ole' lady.

And then you have the standard club girl. The one that just loves sex and loves how an outlaw biker gives it to her.

So, Hallie was known as a kutte chaser. She was found poking needles through Whit's condoms and that was a big ass no-no.

Hell, I was surprised that they didn't end her, but I do know that they locked her in the basement three weeks ago and had her blood drawn every week to ensure that she wasn't pregnant.

They just carted her off the property two hours ago.

I was brought back to the here and now when Stella started to explain the man she had called Pipe to me.

"He's been a nomad for going on three years now, I think. His wife made a big ordeal about a run he went on and got hurt and she cried those fake ass crocodile tears. Anyway, to shut her up he went nomad and spent time with her. But she didn't care that he lost all the protection he had and when he got hurt again because ten guys jumped him, she was like *oh my gosh I didn't realize, let's go back*. Fucking cunt muffin. Anyway, so that's why he's back."

I nodded then.

And he is off-limits. Good.

Because I never envisioned myself ending up with any of the brothers. I just wasn't like that, but for that man, for Pipe? Hell, I would be tempted to do anything to keep him in my bed under lock and key.

But I did want to know how he got hurt and knew that the run he was on wasn't any of my business, so I asked lightly, "You said he got hurt? Where?"

She raised a brow at me. I smiled and shook my head, "Not *where* did he get hurt. Where on his body did he get hurt? I know I am not allowed to know anything that happens. It's club business. I get that you know things because you are the president's daughter."

"And that statement right there is why I wish you hadn't become a club girl." The breath in my lungs stalled when Asher said that as he walked into the kitchen.

Cocking my hip to the side, I asked, "And why is that?"

"Because you would have made a killer ole' lady." He said as he pressed a kiss to Stella's cheek and said, "Be back in time for dinner."

"Okay, Dad." She smiled at him and then started getting out things for dinner.

I didn't know that anyone else was in the kitchen with us because my back had been to the entryway.

But when I heard that deep rasp again?

Shivers coursed down my spine.

"I got shot in the calf while I was riding, didn't go to the hospital as I should have. Got infected, and now I have a limp. Got jumped, five broken ribs, collapsed lung, concussion, and a broken femur." And with that, Pipe walked over to me.

The air in the kitchen suddenly turned down. Stella faded into the background when he stepped toward me, looked down, and quirked his eyebrow.

Without saying a word to me, he reached his hands down and finished buttoning the last three buttons on my cover-up, and not once did he lose eye contact with me.

Then, without so much as another word to me, he turned and walked out of the kitchen.

If I told you that I didn't watch his fine ass hugged tightly in those denim jeans, I would be a liar.

A big fat liar.

If I also told you that I was glad he was married, I would also be lying about that too.

Married. Married. Fucking married.

## Chapter 4
### Pipe

Standing there as I watched the party raging on, my eyes scanned for the woman I had seen and met earlier today.

I'm not going to lie; my dick had gotten rock fucking hard a-fucking-gain when she bumped into me. And then, it got even harder, if that was possible, when I had breathed in her scent as I finished up the buttons on her cover-up.

And then like a fucking moron, I turned from her and walked out of the kitchen. If I would've stayed there, feeling the soft flesh my fingers grazed over another second longer, I would have broken every single vow I ever made to my wife.

My eyes trailed over every single female here and I'm not going to lie, I frowned when I didn't see her.

"What the fuck has that frown on your face, brother?" Asher, my Pres, asked as he sidled up next to me.

I wasn't one to beat around the bush, so I told him, "Saw a woman earlier, wanted to meet her, get to know her but I don't see her."

Asher didn't even look around, not when an all-knowing glint entered his eyes. "You were looking for Gabby."

"That's what your daughter introduced her as to me, yeah." I nodded, then took a sip of my lukewarm beer.

"Gabby is a club girl. And you need to look for another one if you are looking to get some."

I wasn't planning on cheating on my wife, even though I knew that's what she was most likely doing right now. Why she felt the need to feign a headache after she got a text message I didn't know. All she had to do was tell me she wanted to leave, and I wouldn't have cared. Not. One. Fucking. Bit.

But his statement caused something in my brain to short circuit. Did someone already have a claim on her? Unable to contain the growl that slipped out, I asked, "Why is that?"

He smirked at me and said two words, "You're married."

"And?" I asked him stupidly.

"Gabby had one condition when she came here. And we all took a vote and honored it. She won't sleep with a taken man. It's why she's watching the kids tonight. She has no way of knowing if another visiting brother is taken or not."

And that right there, that simple fact about her, intrigued me all the more.

I wanted to get to know this woman. I wanted to find out what made her tick, what made her smile, what made her laugh, what made her throw caution to the wind and just live life?

I thought I would have to wait another day for that to happen and then, low and behold, the woman that has been on the forefront of my mind walked out of the clubhouse. She scanned the area, and then when her eyes landed on me and Asher, she made a beeline toward us.

Waving and smiling at those that called her name.

As soon as she reached us, Asher smiled down at her as she said, "All the kiddos are asleep, your girl is in there with them, shooed me out of the room and told me to go enjoy the party because Chloe joined her a little bit ago. If it's okay with you, I want to visit some of the ole' ladies. I don't get to see them that much."

"You said Chloe is here?" He asked her and had I not been watching this man's face; it would have seemed like he was just asking to know who was in the clubhouse. However, that's not what it was, oh no.

"She is. She's also in those tight shorts you told her not to wear anymore out in public." Gabby said with a smile she had to force to keep contained.

Asher didn't say a word as he growled and stomped away from us in the direction of the clubhouse, and that caused the woman that was still standing here to laugh uproariously at him, which caused him to toss up his middle finger at her.

"Wanna tell me what all that is about?" I asked her.

"Pres has a thing for Chloe and she for him, however, neither one of them will act on it on account of her age and she is his daughter's best friend."

"Shit," I said with a rasp because I was inhaling the scent that was wafting from her. Fucking blueberry pancake was what I was smelling. And damn if it wasn't my favorite breakfast.

Never once have I ever wanted to bottle up a scent and have it on my sheets more than I did right then and there.

When she looked up at me, I was once again struck speechless, just like I had been when she ran into me, and I finally got to see those eyes.

And when I felt the full force of her gaze on me.

Holy. Fucking. Shit.

She had eyes the likes of a color I have never seen before.

They were blue, sure, but they were *blue*.

The fucking color of indigo.

And that just became my new favorite color.

But first, I had to know, "Are they contacts?"

Please. Fucking please don't let them be contacts.

She chuckled then, which I added to a sound I wanted to hear for the rest of my life. "Nope. They are my natural eye color."

Just as she said that her name was called. She turned her head and as I watched her take a step in that direction, then she stopped, her body went rigid, and I wanted to know what the hell was going on.

Looking over her head I saw that her body was pointed toward Sutton who was sitting in a chair beside Irish and watched as a woman walked over to him and like a little puppy, he stood, not one glance in Sutton's direction, and left.

Then I heard Gabby call out, "Pagan?"

Pagan appeared immediately and even though I couldn't hear what was said I saw him nod. He walked over to where Sutton was sitting, held his hand out, and took her to the main room of the clubhouse.

Gabby looked back at me and winked.

I'm not going to lie. It took everything I had in me to physically restrain myself to not grab hold of her arm and hold her right there at my side.

As I watched her walk away, I knew one thing for sure – Gabby didn't walk in a sultry way to gain attention. She didn't fucking have to because she already had it.

In spades.

Feeling my phone vibrate in my kutte, I pulled it out and watched as one of the cameras in my wife's bedroom alerted me that there was movement.

Pressing record on my phone, I watched for a split second as a man walked behind her, stripping his clothes.

On that, I shut the program down, knowing full well that it would continue to record what was going on.

Taking a sip from my beer, I noticed a woman that I had seen earlier was now walking over to me, and she… well, let's just say that one look at her, and you knew she was a club girl. Not the same with Gabby. Far from it.

"Hi, Pipe, I'm Lizette. We haven't met yet, but I wanted to let you know, if you ever want to feel my body beneath yours, I am game." As she said that she ran her hand up her chest and ran circles over one of the hardened nipples that were peeking out through her t-shirt.

I shook my head and stepped away from her because her scent invaded my nostrils and I wanted to puke. "I'm married," I told her and stepped around her to make the rounds.

Seeing that Gabby was sitting with some ole' ladies and laughing with them, well, that surprised me.

Normally, ole' ladies don't converse with club girls like that. But I knew most of the women of Wrath MC did. They were a different breed.

I was headed towards the table where Knox, Garret, York, and Cotton were gathered, which was at the table right beside theirs when Fiona jumped up and ran over to me.

Smiling, I opened my arms for her and the moment she was in them she hugged me tightly.

Glancing over her head, I looked at Knox and received a chin lift.

He didn't let many people hug his wife.

But he allowed me because of an incident involving his son a year or so ago.

Some stupid punk thought it would be funny to tackle him and somehow take his prosthetic from him.

I had been in the area, and they had been on a run.

I still didn't know why they had called me, because after I finished beating the dog shit out of the guy who had done it, Knox's daughters, Kiiri and Kynnydee had rushed over and delivered their own brand of an ass-kicking.

Normally, when you stick up for a kid, they rebel against you. But not Kase.

No, after I had handed him his prosthetic back, and he put it back on, he offered me his hand. Then he pulled Kynnydee and Kiiri off the guy, gently mind you, and then he swung one arm. The sound of his fist crushing the guy's windpipe. Well, that was a sound one never forgot.

The cops had been called, and a paramedic was rushing over when Kase called out, "Crushed windpipe."

"Thank you for what you did for my son," Fiona said again. This happens every single time she sees me.

"Think nothing of it." I hadn't realized that she had pulled away and had looked to where my eyes were aimed at.

"Ahh, Gabby."

Lowering my voice, I asked, "You know her?"

She nodded, "She's a sweetheart. The first time we met her, she ignored our men, took in our kuttes, and held out her hand. She told us her name and said she would never come on to any of our men because they were taken. She didn't want us to ever worry about her if our men were on a run and they stopped here. She's a keeper. That's for sure. I know most club girls never get claimed, but she's one of the ones I wish that would."

And that single statement was the start of my complete fascination for the woman.

I smiled when Fiona winked at me and then walked over to the ladies and then said something to them. Each woman nodded, going to their men, which opened a seat right beside Gabby.

Was I going to waste my chance of getting closer to her?

Of inhaling her scent?

Of breathing in everything that is her and committing it to my memory?

No. No, I sure the fuck wasn't.

And that was how I spent the rest of the night, sitting there beside Gabby. It was later in the evening when I watched as Irish walked back out of the clubhouse straightening his clothes and searching the courtyard.

Apparently, he didn't find what he was searching for and when his eyes landed on Gabby, he walked over to us and the moment he reached Gabby he asked, "You seen Sutton?"

She nodded, took a sip from her beer, and said so nonchalantly that he couldn't tell that she had a hand in this, "I saw Pagan take her into the clubhouse. That was hours ago. You need her?"

I brought my beer to my lips to hide a smile that was forming on my face.

"What did he need her help with?" He asked her.

Gabby hadn't said that he needed help with anything, oh my brother was a dickhead.

She simply shrugged. "Not sure, but well, she liked whatever he said to her. She jumped out of her chair lightning quick."

I watched as Irish's neck turned beet red in color, his nostrils flared. "You mean?"

Gabby sat her beer on the table, then leaned on her forearms, "You know me, Irish, you know I'm blunt and tell it like it is, so I don't want to hear a single word for disrespecting you for what I have to say. Everyone knows how she feels about you. Everyone also knows how you act whenever another brother even talks to Sutton. We also know that whenever that other woman comes here, you drop Sutton like a hot potato. It's not fair to Sutton. Make a choice. Because it happens again, and you won't just have a pissed-off Sutton to deal with."

Irish opened his mouth to say more but I saw Pagan and Sutton walking back into the courtyard, and Sutton, well, she was glowing.

Irish turned his head and then bellowed out, "The fuck did you do?"

Pagan crossed his arms and glared at Irish.

But it was Sutton that put his ass in his place, "Went for a ride. I'm surprised you're done with your whore already. Normally, you spend the night with her in your bed. Hope she realizes how special she is. Cause even I don't get that." And with that Sutton shoulder-checked him then winked at Gabby and mouthed *bike ride*.

I saw Gabby wink at her and then I wanted to slam my fist in Irish's face for what came out of his mouth next. "So what, my dick wasn't good enough for you now? You whore."

Sutton stopped in her tracks and turned stiffly towards Irish, and I saw it in his face, he knew he fucked up, but it was too late. "Last time I checked ever since I joined the MC, it's only been your dick that's been in my mouth and in my pussy. But my body sure as hell hasn't been the only place your dick has been. But, after that bike ride with Pagan, he wants to fuck me seven ways to Sunday? I just might let him. Oh, and the last time I checked, I know I've been with one man willingly my whole life, and that's you. I bet your whore can't say the same, and neither can you. So, watch who the hell you call a whore. And if you ever call me one again after what I went through a year ago, I'll kill you."

You could've heard a pin drop as Sutton stormed to the side of the clubhouse and left.

I was up and making my way to Irish to beat the hell out of him, but it was Rome who beat me to it and punched him square in the face.

"We all know what that girl went through. She was raped. And you have the nerve to call her a whore. The only reason none of us have even tried to be with her was that you were the only one she trusted."

And with that, Coal walked up and punched him in the kidneys.

I stepped up and brought my arm back, and I sailed it into his other kidney. Smiling at the pain on his face.

And by the time everyone got a hit in for how he treated Sutton, the man was limping back inside the clubhouse.

I only knew about what happened to Sutton because Asher had called me to ask me what I thought.

She needed a safe place, and we were that.

## Chapter 5
### Gabby

Was this really happening right now?

Holy fucking shit.

Not to mention the anger and jealousy that had risen inside of me when Fiona, God love her, had done nothing but run to Pipe and wrapped her arms around him.

But watching him punch Irish in the side for the words he had spewed at Sutton. We all knew what had happened to her.

But that is her story to tell.

And as I watched Pipe grunt in satisfaction as he made his way back over to the table, I couldn't help but remind myself.

Married.

Married.

Married.

It was frustrating that I had to keep chanting it to myself to remind me of that fact that I freaking hated. Because I can promise you, feeling his hard body against mine when I had bumped into him earlier today? I wanted to feel that again. Everywhere.

Every line.

Every plane.

Every muscle.

I wanted to feel his heartbeat beneath my head.

I wanted to take all of him in.

And then it happened... he took the open seat next to mine.

Lord have mercy, the man's cologne.

"We haven't officially met, I'm Pipe." He told me as he held his hand out to mine.

Shaking my head, knowing I was going to regret this, I held out my hand and placed it in his.

And the moment our skin made contact? I felt it... a surge of electricity raced up my arm, and his eyes had widened at that too. I wasn't the only one.

Clearing my throat, I said, "Hi, Pipe. My name is Gabriella, but everyone calls me Gabby."

He shook my hand and then that's when I saw it, the reluctance to do something, and then he let my hand go, fisting his and placing it on his thigh.

"Why does everyone call you Gabby?" He asked me.

"They said Gabriella was a mouth full." I laughed as I saw Pagan walk by and called out, "Hey, Pagan!"

He stopped in the direction he was walking in and then stepped over to me, smirking and saying, "You change your mind?"

I laughed at him. "No, I am still off, but remember that favor you owe me from two weeks ago?"

He smiled and shook his head. "Yeah. I do. What do you want?"

"Can you grab me a beer?" I asked him and batted my eyelashes at him, which, for some reason, caused a growl to come from Pipe. That was fucking weird.

"Of all the things you could've asked me for, you want me to get you a beer?" He looked at me while he shook his head.

I nodded and shrugged. "You know me, Pagan."

He shook his head and headed to the coolers and grabbed two beers, one for me and one for himself, apparently.

He handed it to me and held onto the bottle, not letting it go just yet. "This doesn't make us even, darlin'. You call that favor in whenever." And with that, he let the bottle go.

And before I could open it, Pipe reached over and twisted the top off for me. I muttered my thanks and took a long pull of the amber liquid.

"What favor did you do for him?" Pipe asked, and me not knowing that everyone at the table was watching and listening intently, I opened my mouth to answer him.

"I'm sorry, but I can't tell you what that was. That's up to Pagan to tell you."

"You do realize you're denying a brother, right?" He asked with a growl in his tone.

I nodded. "Yeah, I know that, but if you bring the matter up with Asher, he will take my side because I am defending a brother." I told him as I took another pull from my beer.

He didn't push anymore, but what he did do was shock the shit out of me when he slammed his beer bottle down on the table, stood up and walked over to Pagan.

"That boy has it bad for you," Novalie said with a twinkle in her eye.

I shook my head. "Novalie, he's married."

"Honey, we all know how you are, but we also know that his wife is a complete bitch." Knowing that he was married to someone that Novalie would label as a bitch, I didn't need to know anything else.

I turned my head to see that Pagan had nodded, and then looked at me and winked.

Pipe was back in his chair, beer back in his hand as he looked… happy?

"Find out what you wanted to know?" I asked him as I smirked.

He looked at me and smiled, oh there went my lady bits. "Yeah, he told me that you could've told me, but he was honored that you didn't." I shook my head and laughed.

"What was it?" Valerie asked from her place beside Garret.

"Some fucking deer ran out in the middle of the road, and he laid his bike down, and in doing that, he had his insulin in his saddlebags. Fucking ruined his bottle of insulin. So, Gabby here got in contact with a friend of hers and got him another bottle. He's type two diabetic."

"That's not something major though, you could've told him," Marley said from where she sat on York's lap.

I shook my head. "No, I couldn't have. If he would've asked me before Pagan became a brother, then I wouldn't have had a problem telling him, but he's due respect now. On top of that, I don't know if the brothers know about it. I wouldn't disrespect him that way." I said, as I took a pull from my beer.

"Respect that," Cotton said with nods from Knox, Garret, and York.

"Y'all think of pulling her away from this clubhouse to work for y'all, I'll kick your ass," Asher said as he apparently heard the conversation and left that hanging in the air.

Laughter surrounded the group of people.

But I didn't miss the fist bump between Pipe and Asher either.

Just then I smelled something that got on my fucking nerves. Fucking Buster was walking over to us. I couldn't help the sneer that formed on my face. "We don't like him?" Valerie whispered.

I shook my head, then whispered, "You'll find out why."

Just then Buster sidled up next to me and did that creepy thing of running his hand along the back of my neck, "Looking good, darlin'."

"Thanks, Buster," I muttered, trying not to sound like his touch disgusted me.

All the while ignoring the low growl that came from Pipe. I didn't even want to touch what was going on with that.

"Asher said you were off tonight… but I don't think we can call it as you working. I'll even do all the work."

"No, Buster," I said in a low tone.

He leaned into my ear and said, "Come on Gabby, please." Which caused shivers to race along my skin.

"No, Buster," I told him for like the millionth time, putting more force into my words.

"And why not?" He asked with a slur in his tone.

"Because you are married," I emphasized on the married bit. But as always, it wouldn't do any good.

Shaking his head, he said, "I'm not married."

It took everything in me to not laugh in his face. "You have an ole' lady. Same freaking thing."

And that was the God's honest truth. If you had an ole' lady in the eyes of the club, she was your wife.

However, if you just had a wife and didn't make her your ole' lady, that was different.

Means you didn't offer her the protection of the club.

Sure, the brothers would help you out when you asked.

Yes, they wouldn't let you be harmed.

But they wouldn't throw themselves in front of a bullet for you.

They wouldn't give up their seat at the table for you either.

"Man, can you show me that new bike you got?" Pipe asked with a take-no-nonsense tone. I knew he was trying to get Buster away from me.

Just then Buster looked at him and then at me, sneered and swaggered over to Asher, raising his voice so everyone could hear what was going on.

Asher took him by the arm and led him inside the clubhouse.

Thank God.

"Now I see what you mean," Valerie said, as she scowled at Buster's back.

"It's getting on my nerves," I told them as I took a pull from my beer.

That was when Pipe asked, "Is it true?"

Raising an eyebrow at him, I asked, "Is what true?"

"You don't sleep with men who are taken?"

"Yes, it's true. If I know they have an ole' lady or wife, they don't get in my panties." I told him honestly.

What I didn't know was that with that one statement, a series of events would unfold.

And I wasn't given a choice in the matter.

Just then Asher stepped out of the clubhouse and called out, "Gabby?"

I looked up at him and gave him my full attention. "Yes?"

"My office." He said as he turned around and walked back into the clubhouse.

Looking around, my eyes landed on Chloe, who wore her little heart on her sleeve.

She was so in love with that man it wasn't even funny.

Nodding, I stood up and waved at the ladies and walked around Pipe, not knowing he had followed me seconds later.

Following Asher into the clubhouse, down the hallway, and to his office, I asked, "Is this a closed-door meeting?"

He shook his head. "Look, not sure what Buster's problem is, but he keeps pushing it with you. Anything you're doing? Teasing him? Anything? Because it's not often that a brother goes against something we voted on."

I shook my head at him. "No, Asher. In fact, every time he tries to touch me, I move away from him. Hell, every time he comes near me, I try to find an excuse to get away from him. I don't know what his deal is honestly. And I keep telling him no because he has an ole' lady."

"Never known you to lie, darlin'." He said with a sigh.

I nodded my head. "Yes. You know I hate that. But Buster knows this, everyone knows this. When I came on with y'all, I made it a point that I wouldn't sleep with someone that has an ole' lady or someone that is married. I was very adamant about that fact. Y'all agreed with me. He was in the room when the vote took place. If he didn't like it, he should've said something."

"He probably figured you would change your mind," He sighed then and pinched the bridge of his nose. "If you didn't have the tightest pussy I have ever felt, I would tell you to kick rocks. Women, too much fucking trouble, I tell ya."

I smirked at him, "I wouldn't do that to Chloe, so I would even tell you no now."

He chuckled, "Alright, I'll have a talk with him and remind him of the vote he agreed to. You're lucky I respect the fuck out of you. But if he doesn't stop, and you know good and well he's going to keep at it, you might have to leave the club, darlin'." I knew he respected me for my determination to not sleep with a married man, even if he just had an ole' lady, it was the same in my book. And that was because his wife, Stella's mother, had cheated on him in the worst possible way. She did it with his brother. His blood brother. And as far as I knew, they still haven't spoken, because after Asher had beat the hell out of him, he ran. Like a little bitch.

    I nodded, then turned and walked out of his office and ran into Pipe, who was leaning against the wall with his arms crossed over his chest. "I wanna get to know you. If what my gut is telling me is true, then you won't be leaving the club. You also won't be a club girl anymore."

    I didn't respond to that. Instead, I had something I needed to do first.

    Walking out of his office, down the hall, then out to the party with Pipe at my back, I made a beeline for Chloe and whispered in her ear, "Nothing happened with me and Asher. And nothing ever will again."

With that I winked at her and headed back to the table with Pipe still at my back, not knowing that all the while there was a woman who had just come back to the clubhouse that I have yet to meet and someone else who had his eyes trained on me protectively.

# Chapter 6
## Pipe

Something else I didn't know, something that I have never experienced, or even seen in all the years I've been breathing… that instant feeling when your soul recognizes its other half.

Sitting there beside this woman who was so confident in who she was.

Someone who exudes this light that I would give my last breath defending, never allowing it to even dim.

And should her light go out? There is that deepest, darkest part of me that I always keep a tight rein on. Well, that motherfucker would be unleashed.

It was almost as if she had sucked me into her little bubble because I didn't notice anything else going on but her.

Not the way Chloe's eyes had trailed after Asher.

Not the way Coal had grabbed Adeline and taken her off somewhere that was darkened.

Not the punch that Irish had landed in someone's jaw when he had grabbed Sutton on the ass.

Nor the woman that was shooting daggers at me and a sneer at Gabriella before she left.

"Gabriella, wanna play twenty questions?" I asked her. The truth was, it was the only way I knew how to find out stuff about her that I was dying to know.

"Sure, will you answer something for me before we play?" She asked me after she took a drink from her beer.

I nodded and took a swig from my beer. "Ask it."

"Why do you call me Gabriella instead of Gabby?"

"Because Gabby doesn't suit you. Not of the woman I've seen. But Gabriella, yeah, that suits you. You're something else, darlin'."

"That was a good answer, Pipe," Novalie said as she leaned into Cotton.

Then Valerie had to pipe in with, "I wanna play, too."

Was there a nice way to tell the ole' lady of the enforcer for Wrath's mother chapter that this was an a and b conversation and to c her way out of it nicely?

However, I didn't have to be an asshole because Garret had obviously read the displeasure on my face, grabbed his woman up, and took her to the other side of the party.

And with that, everyone else got up and left, too.

Then I felt bad, well that was for all of two point five seconds because the woman at my side threw her head back and laughed.

And let me tell you something, I've never seen a more gorgeous sight than that right there.

Never in all my thirty-five years of life.

After she had her laughing fit, one that I just sat there and took in and marveled at her, she looked at me with that all too familiar twinkle in her eye.

"Your turn," I told her.

"Why are you still here if your wife isn't?"

Damn.

"Starting with the big guns I see." I couldn't remove the smile that formed on my face, even if I wanted to.

And her reaction? Was to just shrug. Fucking shrug.

"Want the answer that's a lie or do you want the answer that's the truth but will make me come across as an asshole?"

She quirked an eyebrow at me, "The truth. Always."

"Because my wife is a bitch, and when she left earlier, it wasn't because she had a headache, it was so she could go screw someone in her bed in our house. Never had a reason to not go home and sleep in my bedroom alone like I always do. Not until I saw you earlier today."

She processed that, then she held up her beer bottle to me, and not knowing what to do, I clinked mine to hers as she said, "To all the skanky hoes who need to catch a venereal disease and die."

"Cheers to that." I told her, took a pull from my beer with her, then asked, "Why won't you sleep with a married man, given what you do?"

"Because my mother made it a habit of doing it when I was younger. I was categorized as a homewrecker when I was only five years old. Made a promise I would never be like her."

What the actual fuck? "How would you even know about that at five years old?"

"Because there are some assholes in this world, about seventy-five percent of the world's population are assholes. I was made aware that my mother was a homewrecker and after seeing wedding rings on the men's hands that walked through our revolving door and had never bothered to take them off, you learn."

And that was how I found out her favorite color, her favorite brand of chocolate, and the location on where to buy her favorite fudge.

That was also how she learned my favorite song, my favorite movie, and the fact that I am deathly afraid of needles, but I have tattoos on almost every part of my body. That was also how she just placed herself as my top priority without even realizing it because, after the talk about her mother and her childhood, she initiated those topics.

So, when I got home that night at three in the morning after I walked her to her room in the clubhouse, my wife was still up and sitting on the couch watching *Real Housewives of Beverly Hills.* She stood up, walked over to me, and sniffed me.

"You don't smell any different." The fuck was this woman on?

"Why the fuck would I smell any different?" I hadn't meant to growl out that question, but it seemed lately I was doing nothing but growling.

She scoffed, fucking scoffed, and said, "Because you were with that slut all night, weren't you?"

It took everything in me to not say that I wasn't the cheating whore in this relationship, but I didn't. Even though I wanted to so badly. And I almost reacted to her, almost, not because she tried to say I cheated on her, but because she called Gabriella a slut.

Instead, I turned from her and headed to my room, and unable to not say it, I stopped and said, "You don't even know me at all."

"I know you better than you know yourself. I am your wife, after all." Wasn't that a crock of shit?

Wanting to prove my point, I crossed my arms over my chest and asked her, "What is my favorite color?"

She smirked then and said, "Black."

Shaking my head, I said, "Wrong. It's gunmetal gray." I didn't tell her that the answer to that question had recently changed from that color to indigo blue. The color of a certain someone's eyes I could get lost in.

"So what, okay, I got it wrong. I still know you better."

"Okay, what am I allergic to?" I asked her. Only someone that was so self-absorbed in their own lives would miss this.

"Oh my God, Pipe, you're not allergic to anything." She said as she rolled her eyes.

"Really now? Then why do I always ask if they use peanut oil when they fry stuff?"

She wasn't scoffing now, but she just had to prove to herself that she thought she knew me with what she said next. "Because you don't like the way it tastes."

"I'm fucking allergic to peanuts."

And with that, I turned, walked down the hallway to my bedroom, shut the door, locked it, and stripped.

And there in my shower, I did something I haven't done in twenty years. Yes, I jacked off in the shower, but never have I come in under three minutes. And that was all because I pictured Gabriella smiling at me.

I was one sick son of a bitch.

\*\*\*

It wasn't until two days later that I got to see Gabriella's face again. She had left with a few of the members to go on a run at an allied club, and since the run was planned before I came back, I wasn't needed.

So, while I was sitting at the bar, watching the door every time it opened, hoping it was her walking through the door, one of the club girls watched it and laughed every single freaking time.

"Oh man, I want to know who you are waiting for, even though I think I know, but I doubt you will tell me." She said, and I didn't even know her name.

I wasn't ashamed of it either.

There was just something about Gabriella that I couldn't put my finger on.

Why she had my undivided attention?

How she was able to stop me in my tracks at just the sight of her?

It was almost as if, somewhere in the deepest part of me knew her, yet I'd never met her before.

Something in my gut told me to grab ahold of this girl and never let go.

Sighing, I said, "Gabriella."

She smiled then and nodded. "I figured as much. I don't know you. But when I did meet you, your eyes never strayed far from her. And I know I don't have to tell you that you are shit out of luck with that wedding band on your finger."

All I could do was nod. "She…" Whatever I was going to say was cut off when the doors opened and there she was.

But instead of smiling and laughing, she was glaring at Asher and stomping into the clubhouse, walking right past me and down the hall. The sound of a door slamming into the wall, then slamming closed, reverberated around the clubhouse.

After I turned my head back from watching her and no longer seeing her, I asked Asher, "What the hell was that all about?"

He sighed and pinched the bridge of his nose, "You know some clubs have a rule that if a woman isn't claimed, she's fair game?"

I nodded, immediately not liking where this conversation was going.

"The club we went to also didn't think that they needed to honor the agreement between Gabby and us."

And that caused a growl to start up in my chest, up my throat, and out of my mouth. "Who?"

"The who isn't important. But what is important is that they took affront to Gabby kicking the guy's ass when she told him no and he didn't listen. They demanded we hand her over to them for retribution."

"And she's here, so I'm guessing you told them to kiss your ass?" At least that's what they better have told them.

He sighed again and shook his head. But it was Whit who answered for him, and the words that came out of his mouth? "We have a week to bring her back there after she packs her things. If she was a sister of one of ours then we would go to war. But she's just a club girl. We all hate it, but it means starting a war we want no part of."

"Then it's time to get that flash drive because I'll be damned if I lose her before I've even had a chance with her. That way I can divorce the piece of shit I married. That means it makes Gabriella an ole' lady. Even so, if any of you try to take her from this clubhouse, the war on your hands from that club will be the least of your worries. It'll be with me. And should they come after her, I'll take them all out and not lose a wink of sleep over it."

Coal walked over to me then and said, "I'll stand with you should they try."

Irish followed him and did the same thing.

"Y'all realize this means war with an allied club, right?" Asher said as he blew out a breath, and then his entire face went white with the next person's words.

"No means fucking no. When did you forget that, Asher?" Chloe stomped past him with Stella following her and shoulder-checking her dad.

"I stand with the guys. Gabby is my friend. You allow them to take her, and I will never forgive you for it." Stella said as she glared at her father while she stomped after Chloe.

"Well, let's hit church. I think I got a plan." Charlie said as he walked over to us and gave me a chin lift.

An hour later, once all the plans were made, we headed out. However, before we left, I saw Gabriella was now back in the main room of the clubhouse as she sat at the bar with the other girls.

And when I passed Gabriella, it took everything in me to not walk over to her and at the very least press a kiss on her forehead and tell her I would be back.

Thankfully, we made the half an hour drive to my father-in-law, Randall's house, and since I knew that he and Rebecca were at a function I wanted no part of, we easily slipped inside.

Charlie had used some kind of program and disabled the cameras, so we wouldn't be seen, and he ran a constant loop of the house half an hour before we got there.

My brothers followed me to his office, and I could tell they wanted to wreck everything and move shit, but no one needed to know that we were here.

We had just gotten the flash drive out of the safe when Asher stepped over to me and said, "Can I ask you a question?"

Raising a brow at him, I said, "Ask it."

"Knowing what you know now about your wife, would you have changed a thing?" I had no fucking clue where he was going with this, but I didn't even have to think about answering him. It all spilled out of me in an instant.

"Honestly, I wouldn't have changed a goddamn thing. Everything that woman did showed me what to really look for in a good woman. And that's Gabriella."

"You claiming her?" Whit asked me as we walked down the grand staircase that was too gaudy for my taste.

"Soon as we get back home, and I get a lawyer started on the paperwork. But yeah, I'm claiming her. She's fucking mine."

"I'll let the other brothers know." Asher nodded and with that, we were out of the house, on our bikes, and headed back to the clubhouse.

## Chapter 7
### Gabby

I was still angry, even after all these hours later, that he had the nerve to get mad at me because I told him no.

Since when did the word no not matter?

And Asher, if I didn't respect the hell out of that man, I would've given him the same treatment as that vile, horrid man. A good kick in the balls and an elbow to his face.

"You okay, girl?" Stella asked as she slid onto the barstool next to mine while Chloe followed suit. Wherever Stella was, Chloe was never too far behind.

"Yeah, just trying to wrap my head around the past forty-eight hours." I smiled at the two of them.

Chloe smiled and said, "Noticed you were walking differently, too. You, okay?"

"Yeah, he elbowed my ribs when I fought back. I'm okay though. Nothing some ibuprofen won't fix." Speaking of that, I pulled a little pack out of my short jeans pocket, ripped it open, and took two with my knock-off cherry limeade that I had seen someone make on a *TikTok* video.

It wasn't long before the other girls joined us, and we were all talking about next weekend when we had a charity run planned.

Just then, the clubhouse doors opened, and I watched as the brothers filed in.

Then something weird happened.

Normally at least Whit, Charlie, Trigger, or Priest would have walked over to me and scooped me into their arms to take me to my room, but none of them did.

I watched as Coal took Adeline, Irish walked over to Sutton who walked away from him before he was even ten feet in front of her, and Whit took Lizette. And as Asher walked over to his daughter, instead of taking the seat beside her, he took the one beside Chloe.

I got what Asher was doing, but with the others? Just what the hell was going on?

But just as I thought that, one man walked over to where I was sitting and smiled. "Gabriella."

"Pipe." I nodded at him.

He got a weird look in his eyes as he asked, "Do me a favor?"

Narrowing my eyes, I asked, "What's that?"

"Go for a ride with me? That's not breaking the rules, is it? Besides, I'm fucking hungry and there's a new place I have been dying to try."

That's when my stomach rumbled. It wasn't breaking the rules, right? As long as there were no romantic relations with him? But, wrapping my arms around him on his bike… I wasn't sure I could handle that. I was prepared to tell him no, that was until he did that thing with his bottom lip. I thought Pagan doing it was cute, but when Pipe did it? Holy hot damn, lord have mercy.

Sighing, knowing that I was going to be in so much trouble later, I asked, "So, what's this place?"

"Backyard Grill." My eyes widened when he told me that.

And if I hadn't been hearing great reviews about that place, I would have been staying my ass in the clubhouse.

Alas, my stomach, and the mouthwatering taste I knew that the place offered, I jumped off my stool and said in a hurry, "Let me change."

In my haste to get dressed, it resulted in him laughing his ass off at me, and my recourse of action… Well, that was to toss my middle finger in the air at him as I rounded the corner, which had him laughing even harder if that were at all possible.

Hurrying, I tugged off my t-shirt and shorts, pulled on my favorite pair of jeans, then rummaged through my dresser doors for my cute top that was peach in color, wrapped around my body, and tied to the side just under my breasts.

Pulling my boots up my legs, I tied them and then quickly ran my fingers through my hair and managed a side braid. Finishing off my outfit was to add a little mascara and eyeliner, and of course spritz on some perfume.

Grabbing my jacket, I was about to rush out of there, then halted and raced to the bathroom to brush my teeth.

After all that was done, I walked out of my bedroom, locking my door, then down the hall and into the main room of the clubhouse.

A couple of whistles and hoots from the guys filled the air around me.

Smiling at them, I noticed that Pipe had sat down on the barstool I had been using and was talking to Asher.

Asher looked over Pipe's shoulder at me and winked.

The moment I reached Pipe, he looked over his shoulder at me and froze.

Nervously, I asked, "Umm is everything okay?"

He looked down at his watch and shook his head. "Less than ten minutes. Takes my wife two hours to get ready for anything. Goddamn."

And I didn't know what to make of that statement.

Suddenly, I felt very self-conscious about myself. Did I not take long enough? Was my appearance not acceptable? I mean, I knew I was pretty enough, but I have still yet to see his wife. So, I didn't know how I compared and why he wanted to spend his time with me.

"Brother, think you need to clarify what you meant," Asher said.

Never taking his eyes off me, he asked, "Huh?"

Asher chuckled then, "What I think he means to say, Gabby, is that he's happy you didn't take two hours to get ready. And not only that, but since he can't take his eyes off you to respond to his Pres, he likes what he sees."

Pipe closed his eyes and shook his head. Opening them again, he nodded and said, "Yeah, what he said."

"Oh, okay. Are you ready?" I asked.

He nodded, then stood and with his hand at the small of my back, he led me from the clubhouse.

When we made it to his bike, he stopped and looked down at me. "You don't mind going for a ride with me?"

I couldn't help the incredulous look that formed on my face. "Are you alright?"

And for some reason, gone was the expressive face from just a few short moments ago, and in its place was someone that was guarding himself, erecting walls to keep himself protected. "Yeah, just answer me. Please."

I had no clue what this was about, but I answered him honestly. "I love being on the back of a bike, Pipe. And for anyone to tell you no, that they don't want to ride with you is a freaking idiot. Even more so when you wear that kutte on your back."

His shoulders relaxed, and he asked, "So you will never tell me no about getting on the back of my bike?"

I hesitated. Because in the future, I would be telling him no. If I was ever claimed by a man, I wouldn't ride on the back of another man's bike, and if I ever became pregnant.

Taking in a deep breath, I smiled a small smile and said, "I can only think of two reasons I would ever tell you no."

I watched as his shoulders tensed, yet again. Just what had this man been going through? "And those are?"

"I would tell you no if I had a man. It wouldn't be right, and if I was pregnant. It wouldn't be safe for the baby." And as soon as I finished, his shoulders were once again relaxed.

Suddenly, my fingers itched to rub his shoulders and loosen them up. There was no way he didn't have knots all in his back from doing that.

With that out of the way so to speak, he continued walking with his hand still on the small of my back, and when we reached his bike, I smiled at the second helmet that was sitting there, "Your wife won't get mad. Right?"

He scoffed, and that was how I understood exactly why he had asked me if I minded getting on the back of his bike. "She's never ridden on it. Or any of my bikes for that matter. So no, she won't mind, and if she does, then she's a fucking hypocrite."

"Okay. So, no questions about her at all. Got it."

He smiled down at me, reached for the black helmet, and held it out to me.

Putting it on, I made sure the strap was tight.

Let me tell you something, there was something about seeing a man climbing on the back of a motorcycle and then holding his hand out for you to help you on.

Then... well, there was that electric spark when your palm slid into his...

Throwing my leg over the back of his bike, I settled in and placed my hands on his sides.

We sat there for a few seconds but then I heard, "This is probably the only time I'll be able to get away with this and it not be against the rules... for now."

And then as my brain had short-circuited on the *for now* bit that had come from his mouth, he grabbed my hands and then pulled my body until it was flush with his and wrapped my arms around his waist.

And damn if I didn't want to splay my hands on his stomach and feel his abs. Feel the ridges. The lines that I knew he had.

With my body against his, he started the bike, that throaty growl rumbling beneath me. There was no other feeling like it. But I knew it wasn't just the bike I sat on that gave me this feeling.

It was the man in front of me.

For a lot of years, I have been searching for my place in life. For my meaning, the reason I was meant to be born.

And the kicker in all of this?

The man that actually gave me purpose, a meaning, one that in his presence, I felt like I was at home? The man that had achieved all of that with conversation and never letting anyone trump the time he was with me, and with those smiles of his? He was freaking taken. Fucking taken.

Reveling in that feeling, I wanted to laugh and cry at the same time for something and someone I knew I would never have.

As we pulled out of the lot, turned left, and the moment that open stretch of road laid before us, he hollered over the throaty roar, "Trust me?"

I didn't even hesitate when I said, "Yes!"

With that one word, he revved up the throttle, and then like a bat out of hell, we soared over the blacktop.

The wind whipped around us, smiling so wide I thought my jaw would crack, laughing when we hit the curves, throwing my hands in the air. Knowing he had this handled? It was almost as if we did this a hundred times, and my body leaned with his instinctively.

Then, almost as if we had been riding for two minutes, instead of the half hour drive, we pulled into the parking lot for the restaurant.

And thankfully the weather was nice out, so they were open.

See, the thing about the place was that you sat on picnic tables that surrounded the grill and everything they needed to make the food. It really was a cool setup.

Not to mention, everything you ate came from the farm across the road, as well as the garden that was nestled next to the restaurant.

It was ingenious too, so if you loved the taste and the quality of the food, you could pick from the garden for your own table at home.

Unstrapping my helmet after he got off the bike, I handed it to him and once he hung it on the handlebar opposite his, Pipe held out his hand for me. "So that's what it's like having someone on the back of my bike."

It was almost as if the ride had caused something to change between us without me even realizing it. Because before, when he wore that guarded expression, I couldn't read him.

But now… now it felt as though my soul has never gone a minute without his in my life.

"I'm the first one?" I asked him, knowing I was.

He nodded.

And the smile that broke out on my face?

Well, there were no words for it.

Pipe's reaction was to wink and throw an arm over my shoulder as he led us to the hostess stand.

And the moment the girl standing there landed her eyes on Pipe, I knew that she was going to try to flirt with him. "Hi, welcome to Backyard Grill." And yep, when she said that, she only had her attention on Pipe. There was also no missing the tone in which she had used either.

"Reservation for Pipe." He said without even looking at her but at the picnic tables.

"I have it right here. For two?" She asked, again not even looking at me and all Pipe did was nod his head then and moved his eyes from the plate of ribs that had just been sat down on one table over to me.

"This place alright still?" He asked.

Wanting to tease him a little, I asked, "And if I said no?"

He shrugged. "Then we will get on my bike and go somewhere else."

"If you think I would choose somewhere else after all the amazing smells that are wafting through my senses? You're crazy."

The hostess butted in and said, "Right this way."

Nodding, I pulled away from Pipe to follow her and had to bite back a laugh when she started to walk in a sultry flirty way.

And when I looked at him over my shoulder, I saw that his attention was solely focused on my ass, and when he looked up at me, his cheeks were pink. He fucking blushed at being caught.

The laugh that ripped out of me had everyone looking at us.

After my laughing fit, I winked. "Besides, I would be a bitch if I told you I wanted to go somewhere else after watching your eyes as they trailed those ribs."

Once we were seated and the hostess made sure that Pipe had everything he wanted, only then did she leave. Now, if he had been mine, I would've said something about it. But it wasn't my place, and that tore through me.

Needing to get out of this train of thought I said, "Five bucks says she finds a way to give you her number."

He smirked, "Ten bucks says the guy that watched you walk over here and hasn't taken his eyes from you will find a way to give you his number."

I scrunched up my brow as I picked up my menu. "What guy?"

He raised a brow at me and asked, "You didn't notice?"

"No. Why would I? I'm here with you." I said as I looked down at my menu.

Pipe was silent for a long moment until I met his eyes and realized he hadn't even touched his menu. Placing my menu on the table, I asked, "What is it?"

He looked away for a moment, then brought those soulful eyes of his back to me. "Anytime I'm out with Rebecca and men stare at her, she flaunts her body more."

"Pipe…"

"I don't want to talk about her. Just, fuck, knew I deserved better, just didn't realize how much until I met you."

I wasn't entirely sure what to say to that, and not wanting to shove my foot in my mouth, thankfully, the waitress came over and impressed me. She made sure to make eye contact with me when she took my order. And not once did she flirt with Pipe.

"What kind of oil do y'all use to cook the fries in?" He asked, which I thought was weird, but who was I to complain when I asked for mustard and ketchup for my fries?

"Umm, I'm not sure but I can ask?"

He shook his head, "I'll just take a side salad with my burger, please, with ranch."

After she took our orders and walked off, Pipe looked at me and asked the question I had been expecting.

"So, tell me, why did you decide to be a club girl?"

"Do you want the short version or the long version?"

"I want the version that you're comfortable telling me and only the truth."

I nodded and unwrapped my straw, then placed it in my sweet tea that the waitress had just sat down.

"I told you about my mother and all of that. Well, I was in high school, and I was getting my toes done before graduation. The one thing I splurged my waitressing money on were pedicures. Anyway, my grades were pretty good, and I had gotten offers to attend college but none of them were full rides. I had half of the tuition saved for community college. My mother, well, she was too focused on finding her next meal ticket. I didn't want to be like her, even though everyone thought

I was nothing more than a gold-digging whore like her. So, when I heard Lizette talking about it in the salon, I walked over to her and asked her about it. Been a club girl for a little over a year now and I've almost got three years' worth of tuition saved up for any college I want to attend."

"I admire the fuck out of that. I really do. But you got me thinking you were a virgin when you went to the clubhouse for the first time. Weren't you?"

I nodded my head. "Yeah, I talked to Asher, and he popped my cherry. I've only been with five men total."

Just then our food was placed in front of us, and he was so right about the food. It was fabulous.

# Chapter 8
## Pipe

    Sitting across from Gabriella, I couldn't help but be amazed.
    Everything about her amazed me.
    The way she ate, the way she carried herself.
    The way it seemed she gave her all.
    Everything about her.
    So, it was no surprise when she got up to use the bathroom that they had in a small building where they housed the cold stuff and I saw the guy that had been checking her out get up and mimic her movements.
    I couldn't tell you how much it ate at me that I couldn't get up from my seat and grab the man by his throat and slam his face into the wood on the picnic table for even daring to look at her, much less for following her.

Instead of eating, my eyes were trained on the bathroom, and when she came out, so did the guy.

I watched from my position as he said something to her, and I saw she wasn't taking anything he was saying to her to heart.

But something he said had her tossing her head back and laughing at him in his face. She shook her head then and pushed by him then started walking back to me.

That was when I saw the man reach out to grab her forearm.

I was up and out of my seat faster than I could blink and was hauling ass over there to her.

But I stopped halfway and just watched the show as it played out in front of me.

The man barely got a hand on her forearm before she spun on him, pulled something from the small of her back, and pointed it at the man's head.

"I told you no. No, I didn't want your number. No, I don't want to see how well you can fuck me. And no, I don't want to see that limp, small pencil dick you have in your pants. I know it's small because only men with small dicks don't take no for an answer. And if you ever call the man I am sitting across from nothing but a no-good biker again, I'll show you why Saturday is my favorite day of the week."

With that said, she walked backward, and when she was a safe enough distance from the man, only then did she give the man her back.

Instead of walking over to me, she walked over to the woman that was in tears and said, "You deserve better than a man that cheats on you. Don't settle for anything less than you deserve."

I was still standing there when I noticed the hostess had something in her hand that she had crumpled up. "What's that?"

"Umm it was my number, but I don't want to piss her off now." And then the hostess was beating her feet back to the stand.

And all I could do was chuckle.

When Gabriella made it back to me, I smiled down at her. "You didn't need me, did you?"

She shook her head but then said something that shocked the fuck out of me, "No, but I am glad that had I not had that handled, you would have, with no questions asked."

"So, do you want to hand me the ten? Because I owe you five." I asked as we both sat back down and finished eating. Which had her chuckling right along with me.

After I paid our bill, we were walking out to the bike when from the corner of my eye I saw that same woman giving that man hell. When she called him a little bitch, I wanted to laugh and shout out you go girl, but when I saw him bring his hand back to smack her across the face, I saw red.

The moment his hand hit her cheek I let out a bellow and then charged the man. I was five steps from him, and then I brought my arm back, and let it sail into the man's face.

Grunting in satisfaction when the man's head snapped back, his eyes closed, and then he hit the ground. Knocked out cold.

Just then I felt Gabriella at my back. She walked around me to the woman and said, "Hey honey, what's your name?"

The woman nodded and said, "Sonja."

"Hi Sonja, my name is Gabby, and this is Pipe. Is there anyone we can call for you?"

She was shaken up and murmured, "My brother, Hammer, please."

I've heard of a Hammer. He was a member of Wrath MC, South Carolina chapter. Couldn't be the same man. No way would that man tolerate his sister being married to this piece of shit.

Gabriella nodded and then handed Sonja her phone. After she tapped the number in, Gabriella placed the call on speaker.

It rang twice, then we heard, "Speak."

"Hi, I'm looking for Hammer. Is this him?"

"You called the number woman."

I growled at his disrespectful tone to Gabriella. "Who the fuck just growled at me?"

"That would be Pipe. My name is Gabby. We were out eating at the same place as your sister and her husband. Sonja's husband got fresh with me. She called him out on it, and he slapped her across the face. Pipe saw it happen and knocked him out. She's shaken up and wanted us to call you."

He asked, "Sonja, you okay?"

Sonja smiled then and said, "I'm okay, Hammer, but I need your help."

"Say no more." Then we heard some shouting and then he was up and moving. That right there was a biker. I was sure of it. "Need me to come to the house or somewhere else?"

Leaning into Gabriella, I said into the phone, "Is this Hammer with Wrath MC, South Carolina chapter?"

He growled, "Depends on who the fuck is asking."

"This is Pipe. Zagan MC."

I heard an inhaled breath on the other end of the line. "Well, fuck me."

"Fuck me indeed. If she's okay with it, she can come to the clubhouse to wait on y'all."

"Got it. Sonja, go with Pipe and his woman. No safer place for you. Hitting the road now."

After Gabriella hung up the phone, I looked at Sonja. "You okay to drive?"

She nodded then, and I said, "Follow us. You need to stop for anything, just flash your lights, okay?"

And with that, we loaded up, hit the road, and headed back to the clubhouse. On the way there I placed a call to Asher and let him know what had happened, knowing he would give me the okay for them to come.

And the entire time back to the clubhouse, neither of us commented on the fact that Hammer had called Gabriella my woman.

Pulling back into the clubhouse, you could hear the rock music from the speakers blaring out some Metallica.

Helping her off my bike, Gabriella undid the strap on her helmet and handed it to me. "Keep it."

She looked at me with an odd expression and asked, "Why?"

I shrugged my shoulders and said, "Because I bought it for you."

Just then I heard Sonja's car door open, and as she got out, she asked, "Is it okay if I park here?"

"Sure is. Come on, let's get some ice on your face," I told her as we all headed into the clubhouse,

Gabriella taking Sonja to the kitchen while I nodded to Asher.

After she had ice on Sonja's face, they both stepped out into the main room, her helmet still tucked underneath her arm.

She walked her over to Stella and said, "Sonja, this is Stella, Asher, the club president's daughter. I'm not an ole' lady, so I can't protect you from any of the men, but she can."

Sonja nodded then and sat down in a chair beside Stella.

Gabriella walked over to me and said, "I'm going to go change into something comfortable." She told me and, like the man I was coming to be where she was concerned, I followed her to her room and waited.

And my idea of what she would put on and hers were two different things. To my soon-to-be ex-wife that was nothing more than a comfortable blouse and slacks.

But to Gabriella, that was a long-sleeved t-shirt and some soft-looking shorts. She was even putting her long, curly hair out of the braid and then did some kind of voodoo crap that had it sitting perfectly on top of her head in a messy bun.

"Ready?" She asked, not even surprised to find me standing there outside of her room.

And all I could do was nod.

Because what I wanted to do was to trail my lips down the side of her neck and nibble the soft skin at her nape.

"What?" She asked with gleaming eyes.

"Nothing. Let's go see what everyone else is up to."

After we settled at a table with Stella, Sonja, Chloe, and Asher, I had a prospect grab us some beers. I popped the top off of one and handed it to Gabriella. The thing I loved about being a biker in a one-percent motorcycle club was that we lived by our own rules, and everyone knew that.

So, we knew the cops wouldn't bust our door down for underage drinking.

Sitting there, I wanted to know something.

After Gabriella talked to Sonja about what her plans were, which included her brother and his club taking her to her house to get her stuff and move to South Carolina, I asked, "Our age difference doesn't bother you?"

She scrunched up her cute button nose and asked, "We're friends. Right? So why would it bother me?"

I needed to know, because if it did, then I was fucked. Truly and completely fucked. "Humor me. Gabriella, please."

Sighing, she asked, "Just how old are you?"

"Old enough. I'm thirty-five. And if you started here just out of high school, that puts you at nineteen."

"Age is just a number, Pipe. I could name ten people right now who are twice your age that act like they are thirteen years old."

"So, you're telling me it doesn't bother you?"

She shook her head then.

And did I hide my smile behind my beer bottle as I took a pull after I said, "Good"?

Why yes, yes, I did.

Thank God the party was still going strong because eight hours had passed by quickly and I could tell that Gabriella was getting sleepy.

That was when the door opened, and Hammer walked in.

Standing up with Asher, Whit, and Coal, we walked over to him, and then I told him the entire story that we didn't share over the phone.

He nodded and walked over to his sister, but first, he eyed Gabriella. "You the woman that threatened to kill him?"

She looked at me, then at him, and nodded sleepily.

"If you ever need me, I'm there." Then he looked over his shoulder at me when Gabriella stood to hug Sonja goodbye and said, "You got a great woman."

And did I correct him? No, I sure as fuck didn't because she was going to be my woman. Come hell or high fucking water, I would be making that happen.

Since it was late, I crashed in my old room at the clubhouse for a few hours because we had a run to make tomorrow to deliver a shipment of AKs to a neighboring club.

And the kiss I placed on Gabriella's forehead before she closed her door still tingled on my lips.

***

I wanted to get back to the clubhouse and see Gabriella. The time with her yesterday did nothing to cool the fire I was feeling for her.

No, it only ramped it up to a hundredth degree.

However, I had signaled to the brothers that I was veering off to head to my lawyer's office. I had already called him this morning and instructed to have everything ready.

And his words were *about damn time* when I signed where he pointed.

After I left the lawyer's office I drove to the house and low and behold, her father's car was there. Two birds, one stone and all of that.

Shutting off my bike, I walked it to the side of the house so neither one of them could back over it and ruin it.

Pocketing my keys, I walked through the garage and into the house, not even bothering to take off my boots. All the while ignoring the two of them talking in the formal sitting room she just had to have and instead headed for my bedroom.

Luckily, all my shit fit in two duffels.

Pulling out my phone, I placed a call to Pagan and asked him to bring a prospect with him to come and drive my truck with my shit back to the clubhouse.

After I had everything packed, I grabbed my two duffels, walked out of my room, down the hall, and sat them by the side door. That was when my soon-to-be ex-wife asked, "Where do you think you're going?"

"I'm leaving. Had enough of this shit. You can either sign these or don't, don't give a fuck, because luckily, I got enough evidence of you cheating to last a lifetime. I'm giving you the house because I don't want this piece of shit. The car is in your daddy's name, and my truck and bike are in my name." And with that, I tossed the papers on the five-thousand-dollar coffee table that she had to have because it has a gold inlay or some shit like that.

"You can't be serious. You are divorcing her because she cheated on you?" Her dad asked me.

I laughed outright at him and shrugged, grabbed my phone, pulled up my photo app, and scrolled down to the video tab, then I handed him the phone.

"Scroll. All the way to the fucking top, I had to get an extra memory card to hold all this shit. There are over five hundred videos of her fucking someone else. And I can promise you, you won't see two videos of the same guy."

His face widened as he looked at her, but did he put the blame at her feet? Nope. He put it at mine.

Handing my phone back, he had the balls to say, "Well then, I guess you don't pleasure her enough."

"We haven't had sex in five years. Wanna know why that is? Because she asked to have sex with two guys and wanted me to watch. If you wanna put the blame on me, that's fine. But your daughter is a whore and I refuse to stay married to someone like that anymore."

Just as those words fell from my lips, I heard the horn from Pagan and the prospect.

Walking to my duffels, I heard Rebecca ask, "Is this because you are infatuated with the club girl?"

"You wanna say that, then yeah. Because it's the truth. She won't sleep with a married man. And I may have just met her a few weeks ago, but I promise you this – she's shown me more compassion, more empathy, and more of a friendship than you have in all the years we've been married."

And with that, I started walking to the door, and I was about to set one of my duffels on the floor to grab the door handle when her dad said, "You do this, and I'll release that video of you."

"Go right the fuck ahead. She's fucking worth it, motherfucker." And I didn't look back.

Not fucking once.

Oh, to be a fly on the wall when he checks his safe and doesn't find the video.

## Chapter 9
### Gabby

The entire morning and afternoon after I woke up, I replayed the events from yesterday in my mind. The restaurant, the ride, the conversation between Pipe and me. Everything.

I knew that they were on a run while we were in the kitchen getting things ready for dinner. And I knew that they had gotten back about five minutes ago because Whit, the asshole, had made a beeline to the kitchen to see what was for dinner.

However, I hadn't seen Pipe yet.

Judging by how he has been with me when he walked through the doors, he would've come to me.

"What's this shit?" Whit asked as he put the peanutless cookie back on the plate and picked up one with them.

"It doesn't have peanuts in it. Pipe is allergic." I said nonchalantly. Trying not to show how weird it was that I paid attention to Pipe. More than I had a right to.

I hoped he was anyway, or I had just made a fool of myself in front of the women by asking them if I could make cookies without peanuts in them.

I noticed that anytime he was here at the clubhouse, he always asked if anything they made had peanuts in them.

Just as I placed another dish on the bar top Asher walked over to me and grabbed my hand. He then pulled me to the side and told me that apparently the president of that god-awful MC that demanded I be returned to them owed Pipe for a few things.

So, he called his marker in and they let everything go.

Funny thing was, ever since Pipe and I got closer, I hadn't even thought about that incident, and I had also let go of the anger that they would have returned me to them.

We were about done with everything, and we were creating a buffet-style dinner on the bar top when I noticed that Pipe still hadn't come to find me. Glancing over at Pagan who was sitting at the end of the bar, I asked, "Where is Pipe?"

I knew that it wasn't my place to ask, but out of all of them, I knew that if it wasn't club-related, he would tell me.

"He'll be here. Had something to take care of first." Just then his phone pinged with a text.

He read it and called out for a prospect.

Then Pagan stood up and said, "He's done. Be here soon." And then he walked out with the prospect at his heels.

Walking over to the girls, I sat down as we waited for Asher to gather everyone so we could all eat.

Thirty minutes later we were lining up when Pipe walked through the doors with two duffle bags, and I let out a breath I hadn't realized I was holding.

I saw him sit them just beside the door and out of the way, and then he searched the main room of the clubhouse.

Like a moth drawn to a flame, the moment his eyes landed on mine, he started to make his way over to me. Getting in line behind me, I asked him over my shoulder, "Why are you standing back here with us? Go up there."

He looked down at me and said, "I'm right where I want to be."

And damn if I didn't have to repeat that all too familiar mantra in my head to remind myself that he was married.

"Okay, why are there two different plates of cookies? What's the difference?" Asher asked us.

"One has peanuts, and one doesn't." Stella said as she grabbed a cookie that had peanuts in it.

Just then Asher looked at all of us until his eyes landed on me and the man behind me, and he smirked. He fucking smirked. I stuck my tongue out at him, which had him laughing as he carried his plate to his table where Stella and Chloe followed soon after.

I felt the man behind me stiffen and when I chanced a look over my shoulder and up at him. Almost as if in awe, he looked at me and said, "I never told you I was allergic to peanuts."

I fiddled with the hem of my t-shirt then. "You always ask if whatever dessert they make has peanuts in it. And at the restaurant, you asked if they cook the fries in peanut oil. So, either you don't like them, or you're allergic to them."

And the smile I was graced with? Sweet baby Jesus.

"I'm allergic to them."

I nodded and started filling my plate up.

And as we made it to the cookies, I grabbed one without peanuts and handed it to him.

He took it from me, ensuring that our fingertips brushed, and took a bite, then winked at me.

I was shaking my head as I went to the table where Adeline and Sutton were sitting as Lizette followed me, and apparently, they had been watching the interaction because Sutton said in a low voice, "That wink and that smile. My God. If I wasn't in love with Irish, I would go after that man."

I smiled and realized I didn't have a drink. Just as I was about to stand up to grab a soda, Pipe walked over to us, handed me one of the two sodas in his hand, and took the seat beside me.

"Thank you." I told him as I opened my bottle and took a small sip.

Coal and Irish walked over to our table, placed their plates down, and grabbed chairs. We all resituated so Coal could sit by Adeline, and Irish by Sutton.

"Is this the claimed but still unclaimed table?" Lizette asked with a laugh, which had all of us cracking up.

Only not for Sutton. I watched with a sad frown on my face as she grabbed her plate, drink, and stood up to leave.

But before she could, Irish snarled, pushed back his chair and walked out of the clubhouse while slamming the door so hard into the wall that the picture frames hanging there rattled.

Sutton sighed then offered us all a smile and said, "I'm sorry, but after his words to me, I just can't stand to be in the same room as him."

I nodded at her as well as Adeline. "Honey, we don't blame you, not one single bit. No one deserves to be spoken to like that, even more so when they know the situation."

Just as Adeline said that, Asher walked over and said, "Sutton, think we need to speak in my office?"

She bowed her head and nodded.

But before she left, Coal said in a low tone, "I'll kick his ass again, you just say the word."

We talked about their situation, funny enough we were all in agreement that Irish needed to pull his head out of his ass or else he was going to lose something we didn't think he wanted to lose.

After dinner, we had cleaned up and I was standing at the bar wiping it down, when I heard, "Hey darlin'."

Spinning around, I squealed and jumped into Taz's arms while wrapping my arms around his neck and squeezing tight. "I didn't know you were coming here!"

With his arms tight around me, he squeezed me right back while walking back to sit on a bar stool. "Wanted it to be a surprise."

Pulling away from him, I looked at his face while saying, "I'm still waiting for why you didn't tell me you were headed this way."

Just then a dark shadow fell over us.

Taz frowned and looked up, and up and then when his eyes settled on the person behind us, he frowned. I didn't have to ask who it was. I knew that man's cologne from anywhere.

"Pipe, good to see you. Heard you were coming back."

Pipe didn't say a word, just growled at Taz and held out his hand. Taz offered him his, and when Pipe shook his head, then looked at me, I got it.

I didn't understand it though. So, me being me, I asked, "Is there something you need, Pipe?"

I felt Taz's chest rumbling against my chest as Pipe looked at me and glared, "Yeah, need you to get off his motherfucking lap right the fuck now."

Suddenly, I felt as though I was playing with fire. Who knew I liked being burned? "And why is that?"

"Because I don't like when another man has his hands on you."

Before I could come back with a reply, something like I wasn't his, and he was someone else's, Tink came into the clubhouse then and said with a shout that only her little body could put out, "Gabby! You're the only woman I will ever allow to be in my man's lap."

Laughing, I jumped off Taz's lap, dodging Pipe, and raced over to her.

Caught up in an embrace, she whispered in my ear, "Who is that fine tall drink of water that's glaring at my man?"

"That's Pipe. I don't have a clue Tink. He's married."

She nodded, then pulled away and looked into my eyes. Seeing the love and the sorrow in them, she nodded again and murmured, "I'm sorry."

Tink was a club girl for all of a single day before Taz scooped her up and claimed her right in the middle of them introducing her. She was the only friend I had in high school. The only one that defended me when all the other kids called me a whore and a gold digger like my mother.

Taz had been a nomad like Pipe was and had settled with a club out west called the Soulless Outlaws MC.

I didn't know what Taz and Pipe had exchanged, but apparently, when we made it back over there to them, Pipe was relaxed.

Tink told me they were headed to see her parents and stopped here on the way.

Sadly, they had only stayed for an hour, and then they left.

It was pushing toward midnight, and we were all gathered around the fire pit outside. After a few more beers with the women, and yes, with Pipe still at my side, he leaned over and said, "Tell me something no one else knows." I wasn't sure how we got on this topic of conversation.

But we did.

And why I opened my mouth and told him something that no one else knows I have no idea.

But in the morning, I will blame it on the half quart of moonshine I swallowed down. Damn, something had to be said about mixing the banana cream pudding with the peanut butter.

"I've never experienced an orgasm unless I was the one giving it to myself." I said it low because the brothers were still around us and that would've been a slap in their faces.

They have been good to me.

I wouldn't do that to them.

I watched as his frame stiffened and I could see that he wanted to say something, but he was holding himself back.

Again, in the morning, I would blame all of this on the alcohol.

"What is it?" I asked him with a slur in my tone.

"Nothing." He shook his head and took a pull from his beer.

"Pipe... please. What is it?"

"You're not going to let this go. Are you?"

I shook my head slowly, knowing that if I shook it too fast, I was going to get dizzy.

He sighed then and leaned over to whisper in my ear, which caused shivers to race along my spine, "Just thinking about all the ways I could make you come with my mouth, my tongue, my teeth, my fingers. Suckling that little nub until it's pulsing in my mouth, then licking up every delicious drop of your come. Giving the same attention to your nipples, your neck, and the backs of your thighs. Wondering if I ran my hands up the insides of your thighs if it would have you screaming out my name with need. Wondering what my name would sound like as you screamed it while I was buried balls deep inside of you."

I had to clench my thighs together to hold in what he was doing to me.

He's married. He's married. He's married.

Gah, this was getting harder and harder to deal with.

The temptation was there.

But I made a vow a long time ago that I wouldn't be like my mother.

That I wouldn't be labeled as a homewrecker.

I was this close to leaving. Because there was no way I could stay after the time we spent together and what he just said to me, and then having to see his wife, the woman I have still yet to meet, to see him doing even a sliver of that to her.

Never would I go back on that promise, that vow I made myself at the tender age of five.

***

It was the next day and Lizette had just stomped over to me from walking past Rachel, Buster's wife.

Under her breath she said, "God! I hate that woman. Why is she such a bitch to me?" Lizette huffed and puffed out a long breath.

I knew she was tired of catching the attitude from the few ole' ladies. I could see her point. She is doing her job by sleeping with the brothers. And I see their point. She is sleeping with a married man.

"See that? They smiled at you and sneered at me. What the fuck gives?"

"You know why," I told her as I locked eyes with her.

"No. I really don't. You're a club girl too, and yet they treat you with respect."

"I don't sleep with men that are taken. You know this."

"Wait... you don't?" She looked at me like I was an alien who had just sprouted out three heads.

"Seriously? You've known me for over a freaking year. When have I ever slept with one of them?

Not to mention, why do you think the taken ones are always calling you over after they've asked me?"

All she did was nod her head and then walk off.

I hadn't realized that I had stopped wiping the bar when Stella asked as she walked over to me, "Hey honey, you okay?"

I didn't know if I was or not, honestly.

Something weird was happening to me.

I missed him.

Those brief moments together, the impact that seeing those smiles form on his beautiful face.

The short text messages I got.

They didn't do it for me.

How was this even possible?

Had she asked me something... oh yeah, I answered, "Just thinking."

"What about?" Sutton asked.

Just as she asked that, Chloe and Adeline walked over and looked at me expectantly.

But it was Stella that tossed her hands up and exclaimed, "Thinking about what girl?"

"Pipe."

They all nodded, and I knew that Sutton and Adeline understood better than most.

I was behind the bar today because the prospects were all tasked with cleaning the bikes to get them ready for a charity run that was taking place this weekend.

It was a run for kids that have leukemia. Since Gage, a member of Wrath MC, Dogwood chapter had fallen for a woman with a daughter that had leukemia but had beaten it like a boss, we were raising money to benefit the other kids that didn't have the help that they did.

All the brothers but a handful were out collecting donations from the townspeople.

Just as I grabbed a beer for Rachel, who sneered at Lizette again, the front door opened, and a woman walked in.

One that had every eye on her.

Who the hell was she?

Was she lost?

Matter of fact, I was about to ask her that when Rachel beat me to it, "Are you lost?"

The woman didn't answer Rachel, just looked down her nose at her and that had me clenching my fists.

She was dressed in pants that I knew cost more than my entire wardrobe, not to mention the shirt that had to have cost more than my phone bill for an entire year.

And don't even get me started on her hair.

That was when the woman walked over to the bar and leered at me.

I was about to go off when she sat down on one of the barstools, looked at the bar top, and then sat her bag in her lap, that I wasn't going to touch the price tag of with a ten-foot pole and asked, "Who are you?"

"I'm Gabby. Who are you?" Something about this woman told me I knew of her, but I've never seen her before in my life. I just couldn't put my finger on it.

What I did know was that I didn't feel bad about that.

Because whoever this woman was, I didn't like her. Not one fucking bit.

With a sneer in her tone, she stated, "You're a club girl."

"Yes, I am. You still haven't told me who you are. Now, is there something I can do for you?" I used the rag under my hand to clench onto it instead of slapping her because she was a rude ass bitch.

"Who I am isn't important right now. I just wanted to get to know the woman that spreads her legs for every man here, uncaring if they are taken or not." Before I could correct her, Gravel's ole' lady Alicia walked over, and with her hands on her hips, she snapped.

"Look, we don't know who you are or why you're here, but let me tell you something, bitch. Gabby here is one of the best. She doesn't sleep with married men. Ever."

The she-bitch huffed out a laugh as she said, "That's a fucking lie."

Gravel's voice boomed when he asked, "Who the hell do you think you are calling my woman a liar?"

The she-bitch finally filled us all in as she crossed her arms over her fake as fuck chest and said rather hauntingly, "I'm Rebecca. I'm Pipe's wife."

Gravel got a disgusted look on his face, one that I didn't understand, and asked with a frown, "Not his ole' lady?"

She threw her hands up in the air and said, "Wife, ole' lady. It's the same damn thing."

"No bitch. It's not. Round here a wife doesn't mean shit. He give you a property kutte? A tattoo? Anything?" Alicia asked and crossed her arms over her chest with an all-knowing smile on her face.

Rebecca shook her head as her shoulders dropped.

Gravel stepped up behind Alicia and wrapped his arm around her shoulders and pulled her into his body.

He nodded and said, "Thought so, bitch. Then round here, you ain't shit. And you won't be coming into this clubhouse trying to pick a fight with one of our girls. Especially when she hasn't done a damn thing wrong."

None of us noticed the club door had opened until a booming voice had everyone snapping their heads to the man that had just walked through the door. "What the fuck are you doing here?"

"Pipe, I've been looking all over for you. I have something to tell you. It couldn't wait. Besides, we need to talk and you won't answer the phone."

He didn't spare her a glance when she said that, instead he had his eyes locked with mine.

I watched as his eyes never left mine as he asked me, "You okay?"

"I'm..." She started, but promptly shut her mouth when she saw where his eyes were trained.

Smack. Dab. On. Me.

In a soft voice, I said, "I'm fine."

"No, she's not. This bitch just accused Gabby of being a whore and that she sleeps with married men, too." Alicia was shooting daggers at Rebecca.

Rebecca growled and snapped, "So what? What else am I supposed to think? You never come home anymore. And when you do come home, you reek of that woman." She said as she pointed a red-painted talon at me. "You're just going to throw away almost twenty years of marriage for that? You're just going after someone that is younger than me? I mean, I get it that we look alike and all but come on. She can't please you.

Why do you want someone that is nothing but a trashy whore?"

I watched in awe as Pipe's entire frame stiffened and then when his rasp came out in full force because he dropped an octave in his tone when he said, "First of all, I know how many men she has been with. I can also tell you that I'm not into her for her age. And you are blind as a motherfucking bat to say that y'all look alike. Y'all look nothing alike. She's fucking gorgeous, as a matter of fact, the first time I laid eyes on her she took my breath away. When I saw you, I saw someone who was an easy lay. And I can also tell you that you're the whore in this scenario. Want to know why I quit giving you my dick? Because I got an STD from you. I haven't been with anyone but you. I also know how many men you've cheated on me with. I quit being able to count them on all of my digits ten years ago. The only reason I stuck my dick in you after that was because I took vows. But after meeting her and seeing that I deserve a hell of a lot more? I'll tell you right now, the number of men she has slept with? Five. Fucking five. So, what does that tell you?"

Trigger walked over to us and told me he needed my help. I chanced a look at Pipe and saw him nod, then and only then did I walk out of the main room and into his office.

And I missed the look on Pipe's face as he watched me and the daggers that Rebecca was shooting at me.

When I came out of his office three hours later, Rebecca was gone and so was Pipe. As were Asher, Charlie, Coal, Irish, and Whit.

Since the prospects were still getting things ready, I took my place behind the bar again.

And for the umpteenth time, I was wondering why the hell none of the brothers have even bothered to come to me like they used to. Sure, it was only five of them, but still, here lately they all treated me like I carried some flesh-eating disease. Hell, even Buster has been leaving me alone.

Just as I thought about that, the door to the clubhouse opened.

And I was glad I had my hands braced on the bar top.

Because of the man that walked through those doors.

Holy motherfucking shit.

He looked good enough to eat.

Gone was the t-shirt he had on earlier and the jeans that were grease-stained.

And in its place was a black long-sleeved shirt, a nice pair of jeans, and his hat was on.

That was when I saw him scan the room, and when his eyes met mine, it happened again. Everyone and everything faded away.

Never once in his trek across the floor to me did he look anywhere else.

I felt the heat emanating from him, wondering what he was up to.

I couldn't get a read on him.

Just what was going on?

But I shouldn't have even thought that.

Because all the words in the dictionary that formed to make those few sentences that fell from his lips… rocked my entire world.

## Chapter 10
### Pipe

And the first words out of my mouth were, "Let's go."

She looked at me with a confusing look on her face and asked, "Umm… go where?"

"Been waiting on you my whole life Gabriella, ain't willing to wait another minute and not know that you're mine and I'm yours."

"You're still mar…" She started to say until I laid the divorce decree on the bar top in front of her.

"After Rebecca showed her ass, Asher told me he had a judge that owed him a favor. Took her and the papers to him and forced her to sign them or else I would share all the videos I have of her cheating on me, and he granted me the divorce. Was waiting on this form." I tapped the decree.

She looked down at it and then back up at me with her heart on her sleeve. "What does this mean?"

"Means I'm free. Means I finally get to claim someone that I know will never cheat on me. Someone who, when I come home, will be there. Means I get to claim a woman that is my other half. Also, means for the first time in my life that after a long day of working, I'll come home to a woman that is wearing a smile on her face. One that's just for me."

She laughed softly then and asked, "You sure about that?"

I nodded. "Damn sure, darlin'."

She bit that bottom lip that I wanted to nibble on with my teeth. "How do you know?"

"I know because when your eyes meet mine, they shine. I know because the moment our skin touched, you inhaled a breath because you weren't expecting it. Know we haven't known each other that long, but when one soul recognizes its other half, it just knows. I wasn't your first, darlin'. But I'll be damned, I'll be your last. And that you can take to the bank."

"What if there's no chemistry?" She asked, and I wanted to scoff.

In fact, I did so and then asked, "Trust me?"

She nodded and then I stepped closer to the bar and held out my hand for her to take. She did so, then I leaned in closer and placed her palm over my beating heart that had taken a rhythm of its own, one I've never felt before. "You were saying?"

She pulled her hand back and then looked up at me with every single emotion she was feeling pouring out of her in those eyes of hers.

I waited for a beat, and then she said those words that split my heart wide the fuck open, "We do this. Means you're mine. I don't share. And it also means I'll give you all of me."

"Honey, in all the years I've been on this earth, I've only ever met one woman that held my attention. One woman that I wanted to lay my heart at her feet. One woman that I want to see swollen with my kids. One woman that I want to stand beside and face anything this messed up world has to offer. One woman that even though this world is messed up, she will make our small world better. Because that's what she lives for. Letting her light shine. And I want all of that. With. You."

"Come to me, baby." I told her and watched as tears trailed from the corners of her eyes and then I had one last option. I looked at Stella and nodded.

She smiled, reached towards the floor at her feet, and brought a bag over.

Smiling, she handed it to me and then tossed a wink in Gabriella's direction.

Eyeing the bag warily, she asked, "What is it?"

"Open it, darlin'." I told her with a smile that I knew I only reserved for her, hell even my ex-wife didn't receive that smile.

I watched as she opened the bag, removed the so-called tuffs of tissue paper or whatever you called it, and then she reached her hand in the bag, and she stilled.

Her eyes snapped to mine. "Is this…?"

I shrugged my shoulders. "Pull it out and find out."

Lightning-quick, she pulled out the property kutte that Stella had made for her.

And that was all my girl needed. She climbed on the bar top, stood, and looked down at me while clutching the kutte to her chest.

I watched as something sparked in her eyes as she said, "Will you catch me?"

"All day every day, darlin'. But I need you to fall at least once. This being in love one-sided thing ain't all that great."

She chuckled at me and then whispered the sweetest words, "How can it be one-sided if I feel the same?"

Grinning, I held my arms out for her to jump into them, and jump into them she did.

Her arms went around my neck as mine went around her waist, and her legs circled my waist.

If those tears of hers were for anything else other than her being happy, I would be kicking my own ass right now. "You're breaking my heart, baby."

When she had her tears all out, she pulled her head from my neck as I slid one hand up to cup the back of her head, and without zero hesitation, I slammed my mouth down on hers. The moment our lips connected; fucking fireworks went off behind my closed lids.

Everything around us faded away and it was just her and me.

The brothers hollering and clapping, the girls with the catcalls.

Guns popping off.

Bombs exploding.

People dying.

Nothing would have registered.

The saltiness from her tears coated my lips, and then when she opened her mouth and tried to get even closer into my body, I slid my tongue into her mouth and the rest, as they say, is history. I lost track of time. Literally.

When we finally pulled apart, we both inhaled much-needed breaths and as her forehead rested on mine, I said, "Now, that's what I call a great first kiss. Can't remember any before that."

"I know what you mean. So do I get to have my name tattooed on you?" She asked as she pulled her head away to look into my eyes.

"Mmhmm, where do you want it?" I asked her as I rubbed my nose along hers, finally getting to do all the things I've wanted to do to her for so long.

She removed one hand from the back of my neck and touched my forehead. "Right here."

I nodded and said, "Make me the appointment."

"You're serious?"

I nodded again, because I sure the fuck was. "Long as you like it, don't give a fuck, baby."

Tears welled in her eyes again and she smiled. "Is there a spot over your heart?"

I nodded yet again. "Been leaving that spot bare for a reason. Never knew why, not until I laid eyes on you getting out of that truck bed a few weeks ago."

Asher slapped me on the back and then asked, "Did y'all want a room?"

My woman? My woman threw her head back and laughed.

She looked at him and said only for my ears to hear, "Are you okay?"

I knew what she was asking me, and to be honest, none of it bothered me, not in the least. "No, darlin', I don't mind. That all happened before you met me. Besides, I lost my virginity to my ninth-grade English Lit teacher."

Her loud, "Eww," filled the room which had me laughing my ass off.

"So, are you going to make me yours in every way? Wife. Mother. Everything?"

"Sure am, darlin'. Just need you to tell me the day after you go to college and graduate."

"But the mother part… well, that's going to have to wait, because as much as I want to slide into your pussy, I got something I want to show you. Need you to get that kutte on, baby. It's why I've been short with you in the texts and the few phone calls we've shared. And we haven't been getting things ready for the charity run that happens next week. They were helping me with something."

She let her legs go, narrowed her eyes at me, dropped down, and then finally I helped her put her with her Property of Pipe kutte.

Damn, did it look good on her back.

I had a fantasy I was fulfilling, and soon.

Her in that?

And nothing else?

Fuck, I was already hard.

Then with a kiss on my cheek, she turned her head and smiled at Stella and asked, "Will you come outside and take a picture for me?"

Stella nodded, grabbed her phone, and followed us, and when we stopped right where the truck had been parked that fateful day, she looked up at me and winked.

And standing there, we took five photos.

I knew for certain exactly where I wanted them to go, too.

After she ran and grabbed her helmet, Sutton nodded and smiled at me. I'd already asked Pagan to ask Sutton if, while we were gone, she could pack up all my woman's belongings and bring them to the house when the rest of the brothers came by for a welcome home party for my woman.

Knowing that I had my forever on the back of my bike? There was no other feeling like it.

And I just knew that with my woman, a lot of firsts were going to be happening and I couldn't fucking wait for them.

The fifteen-minute drive to the property that I bought after I had that first conversation with Gabriella took no time at all. As I slowed my bike down on the gravel drive that I was planning to pave, what I wouldn't give to live inside of her head right now to hear what she is thinking.

But I felt it. Oh boy did I.

Her entire body tightened against my back and her hands clenched on my shirt.

Shutting off the bike, I rolled it to a spot in front of the three-car garage.

Taking my helmet off, I turned my body that she still held on to and looked at the wonderment that brightened her face.

Laughing that after a few minutes she still hadn't moved, I reached up and undid the strap on her helmet, and then hung it on the handlebar.

Wrapping my arm around her waist, I hauled her off the bike and sat her down on her feet.

And I knew that if I didn't have a good hold on her body, then her feet wouldn't have moved, but that wasn't what was on my mind at that moment in time. No, it was that I noticed how her body fit next to mine. Fucking made to fit in the curve of mine.

Like two pieces of a soul connecting as one.

As we made it to the front porch, I knew the moment she saw it, the front porch swing that was painted to match the front door. During one of our talks, she told me that she always wanted a front porch swing so she could enjoy the gentle breeze and have something that she's never had before.

A true home.

Pressing a kiss on her forehead, I led her up the dark gray steps that matched the front porch swing and the front door, as well as the six columns.

Just as I moved to unlock the front door, she stopped following me. Looking down at her, I saw tears in her eyes. "What is this?"

"Well, I couldn't stand the thought of making love to you for the first time in the clubhouse because you deserve so much more. And I wanted to give you a home. One that no matter what, you know you have a safe place to land, no matter what the future holds."

"You did all this? For me?"

"For you? Yeah, I did. Charlie helped me with the deed and shit. And when we get married, your last name will change on the deed. I don't want you to ever doubt my feelings for you. I never gave all of me to Rebecca, but I want to give all of me to you."

"Why? I'm a club girl. None of us entered this thinking we would become ole' ladies."

"Darlin', I don't give a fuck how you became a club girl. I'm just glad you became one with this club. Because had you not done that, I never would've met you, and let me tell you something, that would have broken me down until I'm dead and buried in the ground."

"We've only known each other a short time, Pipe, this is crazy."

"Caiden, darlin', you call me Caiden. I stopped her from doing it when I got my road name. But I don't care if you use it in our house, I don't care if you use it where everyone can hear. I'm Pipe to everyone else but you."

"Caiden, I love this." She smiled up at me. Leaning down, I kissed away the trail of tears from her cheeks.

"Now, suck those tears back, be the confident badass woman I know you to be, and let's go explore our home."

She nodded and when I went to turn the key, she grabbed my forearm and halted me. And for as long as I live, the words that fell upon my ears I will never forget. "Caiden, doesn't matter where we live. All I need at the end of the night is to fall asleep in your arms. Because four walls don't make a home. A person does."

And what happened next?

Well, that resulted in spinning around, bending, wrapping my hands underneath her delectable ass, hauling her up my body, slamming her into the front door, and crushing my lips to hers.

And the loud rumble of bikes didn't break my concentration in devouring her mouth.

It was, however, the loud claps that broke us apart.

"Umm, has she even seen the house?" Sutton asked as she climbed off Pagan's bike and I wanted to laugh at the growl I heard coming from Irish as he watched all of that unfold. Snooze you lose motherfucker.

I shook my head and simply said, "No. She just said something to me that in all my thirty-five years of life I've been wanting to hear."

Shrugging when Gabriella giggled, I pressed a small kiss on her swollen lips, then I unlocked the door to our forever home.

Two hours later after all her stuff was settled in its place in our house, we were all in the backyard grilling out. If I hadn't known that she was perfect for me, the reaction to Sutton packing her stuff would have told me that she was.

Did she complain?

No.

Did she get mad?

No, all she did was say thank you.

Thank you.

That was fucking it.

After we ate the hella good food I said rather loudly, "Appreciate all of you, but it's time for me to finally slide into the woman of my dreams so I need all of you out of here within the next two point five seconds."

And like the good brothers they were, they were up and out of there. Bending down, I placed my shoulder in her belly and strode for the house, making sure I locked the French doors.

All the while she laughed her ass off. "Caiden, put me down."

"That's a big negative, darlin'."

Walking down the hall to our master bedroom, I clicked the door closed with my boot and then I sent her sailing on the bed, loving the sounds of her squeals of laughter. It was music that I never wanted to stop hearing.

## Chapter 11
### Gabby

I have no words for how the man standing in front of me made me feel.

Alive.

Confident.

Amazing.

Breathless.

All those things and more. I couldn't wrap my head around the fact that this gorgeous man wanted me.

He could have his pick of any woman. Yet, he chose me.

Getting on my knees to watch the show that was taking place in front of me, when he went to take his hat off, I stopped him. "Leave that on, please?"

He did nothing but smile at me and nod, leaving his hat on.

First, he toed off his boots and socks.

And I watched in avid fascination as his eyes never left my face while he stripped out of his kutte, then his long-sleeve button-down shirt, followed by his pants, and then there, standing in front of me in nothing but his boxers and that hat.

And oh my freaking God.

Whoever said bikers were nothing but greasy, old, and unkempt? Well, they have never laid eyes on Pipe.

I almost checked my jaw to make sure that I wasn't drooling at the fine specimen of a man in front of me, who, because of my property kutte that I still had on, was mine, all freaking mine.

"You got too many clothes on, baby," Pipe whispered and I winked at him.

"I was enjoying the show." I told him as I started to lift my shirt over my head, but he shook his head.

"Been waiting to unwrap that body since I first laid eyes on you." With that, he climbed up the bed and met me.

Placing a tender kiss on my lips, he placed his hands on my hips, just underneath the fabric, and feeling his roughened calloused hands on my skin, he asked, "May I?"

I nodded and when his fingers brushed the soft buttery material of my kutte. He pushed it off my arms and then whispered, "If you're not too sore after our first time, I want to fuck you from behind in nothing but this."

Now, I've never come with a man. I've never experienced my panties getting wet but twice in my life. The first was when I laid eyes on him for the first time and then just now at his words.

I wanted that. Oh, I so wanted that.

After the leather was off my body and lying beside me on our bed, I held my arms over my head as he took my shirt off.

Then he pushed me backward, my legs automatically coming out from underneath me and going around his body.

First, he unbuttoned my jean shorts, and never did I want to take my shorts off any other way ever again.

Because the feel of his hands running down my thighs and down my calves? Holy mother of God.

Coming back up my body while his lips and fingers left no part of my body untouched, he placed a tender kiss over my heated sex that was still covered with the black lace of my bootie shorts.

Settling over my body, his eyes locked with mine as if we have never been apart. I answered his silent question *are you sure this is what you want* with a nod of my head. And the rest of the night, as they say ladies and gents, was spent experiencing and enjoying new heights, well, that was until I screamed his name.

Our tongues danced to a rhythm that only he and I understood.

As my nails trailed a path along his spine, his mouth blazed a trail down the side of my neck and onto the other side.

And somehow, I hadn't noticed that he had moaned when he realized that my bra matched my panties, black lace, with a front clasp.

And I couldn't tell you where my bra got to.

Because the moment I felt his hot breath on my nipple, I slipped to a place that I have never been to.

Twirling his tongue around my nipple while his fingers pinched my other nipple, I couldn't help my body's response to this, not how my back bowed up to meet his body, not how my heart rate started beating double time.

Moving down my body while kisses from his lips trailed a path to my core, I moaned in ecstasy. This was it.

I was finally getting the man of my dreams on top of me, in me, becoming every part of me.

I wanted to be so embedded with him that you couldn't tell where I ended, and he began.

Was it bad that I didn't want to take a shower after this because I wanted to smell him on my skin?

Then I felt his teeth on my hip, but it wasn't to mark his territory. Oh no, it was to get a good bite on my panties so he could drag them down my hips.

And yes, he repeated the same process back up my body with his mouth, and then it happened.

I felt him swirl his tongue on my clit. And I lost all train of thought.

He worked my clit to a rhythm even I didn't understand. One that brought my body to new heights.

Then, when he left my clit, I whimpered and felt his chuckle against my overheated skin.

But he didn't leave.

Oh no.

I felt two of his thick fingers penetrate me followed by a third, stretching me while his tongue played with my clit, then I felt his fingers curl… and then he tapped my g-spot.

I wasn't aware that I was a squirter.

Not until I felt that release.

And then oh, he did it.

Pulling his fingers out like lightning, I felt him licking up every single drop that came from my body.

Just as I was about to shake my head, to tell him I couldn't stand it any longer, he put his tongue back on my clit, worked it again, over and over, and I saw stars. Fireworks. I came a second time, all with just his mouth and fingers.

Climbing up my body, I felt his heated skin pressing into mine while bright lights danced across my vision.

I heard him ask, "You okay?"

Coming back to the present, I murmured, "Yeah, just never experienced that before."

I saw it on his face. He smiled and asked, "What?"

The shithead. "You're really going to make me say it?"

He chuckled and in a rasp, he said, "Oh yeah."

"Caveman," I muttered as I reached up and pressed a kiss to his throat, loving the saltiness of his sweat.

"Yours." He said as he settled himself between my thighs. "Tell me."

"Never came like that before," I said as I stared up into those dark eyes of his.

I saw the pride shining in his eyes, and then with his mouth lowered to mine, I met him the rest of the way and soon I felt the tip of his uncovered cock at my entrance.

When had he shed his boxers?

But that thought was knocked out of me, along with my breath, as I pulled my mouth from his and stared into his eyes as he stretched me while he entered me.

Stretched me far wider than anyone ever has before.

Not even Asher, and he was the biggest out of the five of them.

He gritted out, "Too big?"

Wanting to mess with him, I asked, "Isn't that your job to make sure it fits?"

He winked at me, pulled slowly out, and then slowly pushed back in and when I started to loosen even more, my man, well, my man moved.

He pulled out of me slowly, then rammed into my body, hard.

I squealed as I grabbed onto his forearms while he pounded into me.

"Fucking holy fucking shit."

"My turn. You okay?"

"Trying not to fucking come. Goddamn you feel, hell, the word magnificent doesn't even describe it."

"Otherworldly?" I asked him as I tried to catch my breath, and then I felt it coming.

But it was unlike anything I have ever felt before.

"Yeah, we… will… go… with… that."

And then he pushed into me even harder, and I was unable to stop it. I felt my body raise off the bed, as my toes curled, and every muscle in my body tightened, and then I was screaming out his name, "Caiden."

"Fuck me." He pulled out and slammed in one more time and he was coming with me.

"I wasn't far away from coming, but the moment you called out my name, I lost my hold on my release."

I couldn't help but laugh at him as I came down from the euphoria that I was feeling.

Only it was to feel him moving in and out of me again.

The entire time as he slid in and out of me, our eyes never lost one another. And as I felt another orgasm building, I shook my head at him.

"One more, baby, do it again for me." He whispered, and almost as if my body had been waiting on his to enter it and take me to oblivion, I came. Hard.

"Caiden!" I screamed as my toes curled, my nails dug into his biceps.

"Fucking hell." He moved in and out of me once, twice, and then he stilled, saying my name, "Gabriella."

And damnit if my body wasn't under his absolute control, I orgasmed again at hearing him coming and calling out my name.

We lay there, spent, or at least I thought I was.

That was until he got this wicked gleam in his eyes and then he reached over me and tagged my property kutte. "Please?"

I stared into his eyes, knowing there was nothing I would ever deny this man. Shaking my head, I asked, "How do you want me?"

"Wearing this, on your knees, your head turned to mine so I can stare into those eyes." He said as he leaned his face into mine and whispered against my lips, "You wanna know a secret?"

Whispering against his lips, I asked, "What?"

"My favorite color used to be gray, weird, I know, but not just any gray, gunmetal gray, been that way since I saw a badass painted truck when I was six.

That was, until you gave me your eyes for the first time. And the color of your eyes became my favorite color."

I did as he asked and then when I felt his thighs at the back of mine and felt him enter me in one long thrust, I moaned.

And suddenly it took everything I had in me to keep eye contact with him.

I haven't always been the biggest fan of sex.

Never had a favorite position until now.

With one man.

With Pipe fucking me doggy style.

"Eyes with me, baby, I want your juicy pussy coming all over my cock."

"I don't know if I can," I said as I fought to not close my eyes.

Gritting out, he said, "You can. Give me one more.'

"That's what you said last time," I whispered.

"I know. But goddamn, you feel so fucking good. May never leave." He told me as he moaned again.

Breathlessly, I murmured, "Can't. You have the club," I sighed as he hit my g-spot once again.

"They keep me away from this body longer than twenty-four hours, you'll hear me saying fuck the club."

"You wouldn't do that," I said. Knowing full well how deep his loyalty to what is his holds true.

"For you? Yeah baby, I would."

And that one statement. Knowing he hadn't said it in the heat of the moment. Well, that touched the deepest part of me. A part that I have kept locked away after watching my father walk out on me and my mom when I was too young to understand that him taking a vacation alone meant that the vacation was never going to end.

But it was the trail of kisses that I felt along the bridge of my nose that brought me back to the here and now. "You left."

"Sorry, just remembered something."

"Tell me," he said as he pounded into me.

"I don't want to ruin this," I said as I felt it building.

"Darlin', the only thing that could ruin this would be for you to stop breathing." And damn if that didn't cause me to lose the hold on my orgasm as my body shuttered all around his.

It wasn't until we were both spent, and he had come again, that we laid there, me on my stomach with his body curled around mine as I felt the wetness seep out of me, and it was gross normally, but with Pipe, I just didn't mind any of it.

Looking into his eyes, seeing the sincerity in them, I opened my mouth and told him, "When I was four, I learned that my father taking a vacation alone meant that the vacation was never-ending. The last I saw of my father was when he looked over his shoulder at me while he carried his bags to his truck and blew me a kiss. After a month of asking where he was and when he was coming home, I quit. Besides, getting slapped across the face every time I asked, well, that really hurt."

"First, what brought that thought on?"

I quirked a brow at his first comment and said, "Because you would be willing to throw everything away for me. Never had that. Not my mother. Not my father. Nobody in my entire life was ever willing to do that and back it up."

He nodded. "Second, what is your mother's name and where is she?'

"She moved to Florida with some business oil tycoon the day I graduated. Her name is Melinda Roberts."

"Third, what's your father's name?"

I couldn't help the chuckle at his line of questioning, and I knew he was going to do something. "Eduardo Costa."

He nodded and then made me a promise that I didn't really need, but it was nice to have, "Promise to make it right."

Shaking my head, I said, "We didn't talk about something."

"What's that?"

"Birth control. I have an IUD. Just so you know."

He nodded. "I know. Already made sure of it."

After we cleaned up and experienced the wonders of getting messy in the shower, again, because apparently seeing my body glistening wet, and able to fuck it, he didn't hold back. I also learned why he had certain steps and rails in the shower. Well then…

However, that night we didn't get much sleep, nope, and that was because we made love three more times.

And it was glorious and wonderful and all-consuming.

And every day for the next month, we woke up together, ate breakfast, and then he fucked me into oblivion. Said that was how he wanted to start his day. Oh, and that was how he wanted to fall asleep at night. Never once throughout the night was he not curled around my body. If I moved, he moved.

Together we rode to the clubhouse, me on the back of his bike, my laptop case in his saddlebag.

And in the main room at the clubhouse, that was where I did my schoolwork. My amazing man had surprised me with a laptop and told me to find the school I wanted to attend and he would cover everything.

So, when I found out that the college that had the best business management program had online classes, that's where I enrolled.

Oh, and we got married last week in a field of wildflowers with Asher presiding over the event. All of which my man just smiled down at me through it all.

And yes, he did tear up when he saw me in my *Marilyn Monroe*-inspired wedding dress from one of my favorite movies, *The Seven Year Itch*.

I was shaken from my thoughts of the honeymoon we had just gotten back from while I was chopping veggies for dinner, when I heard, "I need y'alls advice on something."

We all looked at Lizette and gave her our undivided attention.

"Shoot." It was Sutton who answered first.

"Okay, so Adeline, we all know how Coal feels about you. And Sutton, Irish needs to pull whatever stick he has shoved up his ass out. And Gabby, I love what you have with Pipe. You deserve it. But how did y'all do that?"

I looked at her with a frown and asked, "Do what?"

She shrugged her shoulders as she said, "Capture the men the way y'all have."

Capture?

I guess we did in a way, but I couldn't think of how we captured them, I didn't know how Adeline did that, nor Sutton, nor myself for that matter.

"Why do you ask?" Adeline asked her.

"Because... I want Rome." She said as she had this look on her face, one I had never seen before. I mean, I knew she was infatuated with him, but wanting to be his forever? I didn't know that.

And like the silent man he was, we heard in the open doorway, "Sorry. But you will never have me."

"But... why not Rome? We could be so good together." Lizette said as she tossed her shoulders back and met him head on.

"Because, only one woman I have ever met that has had me wanting to give up this life and be anything she wants me to be, long as she's at my side. And she's not you." With that he turned and moved from the doorway heading back to the main room.

And now we all wanted to know who that woman was. She was a lucky girl, whoever she was.

Irish stepped into the kitchen then and asked, "When will dinner be ready?"

I could see the retort on Sutton's face along the lines of, whenever we get it ready, but Adeline answered for her, "In about half an hour."

He nodded then looked at Sutton who wouldn't return his gaze, then he growled and stomped out of the room.

I knew that it was tearing Sutton apart and I only wanted the best for her.

Irish just needed to pull his head out of his ass for that to happen.

But… I wanted to know what Asher and she had talked about in his office, only, before that could happen, I felt those all too familiar strong arms as they wrapped around my middle.

Whispering, I said, "Caiden."

His lips trailed kisses along the column of my neck. "Never tire of hearing my name on your lips, honey."

"Yo, Pipe, need your help in the shop. I can't get this fucking bolt loose in this truck." Pagan asked him and then with a kiss on the side of my neck, he walked out of the kitchen.

"I just came in my panties. Oh wait, I'm not wearing any." Lizette giggled.

Shaking my head at her, I got back to work chopping up the veggies that we needed for tonight's dinner.

Immediately, I felt a shiver run through me when he walked in through the kitchen. "Hey Gabby."

He's left me alone, ever since Pipe told me that he made it known that he was planning on claiming me as his. "Buster, how are you?"

"I'm good, look I need your help, thinking you were right, thinking you've been right for a long ass time now. I wanna get something on my kutte like Pipe has on his for you. Think you can help me get it on there? Already got it designed and got the patch." And he meant my name on Pipe's kutte.

I looked around for Pipe, and not seeing him, I turned to Stella and said, "Will you tell Pipe where I am?"

She nodded and said, "Got it."

## Stella

I didn't like the look in Buster's eyes. Not one freaking bit.

My dad had taught me a long time ago to trust my gut, that it would never let me down.

And even though Buster was a brother, I didn't want to ignore this feeling that something bad was either about to happen or had happened.

And I wasn't a fool.

Running out of the kitchen, my eyes looked everywhere for either my dad or Pipe.

When I didn't see them, I headed out to the garage because I knew that was more than likely where they would be.

Seeing my dad bent over a bike with Pipe at his side, I raced over there to them.

When I got close, I hollered, "Dad!"

Either it was the fact that I never use that tone for anything other than when I am scared or when something freaks me out, I didn't know, but I watched as his head snapped up. He dropped the tool he was using and started jogging to meet me with Pipe on his heels.

"What is it, baby?"

"Gabby. The girls and I were in the kitchen when Buster came in. He said that she was right all along about being faithful and all this stuff. Asked her to help him sew a patch on his kutte like Pipe did for Gabby. She asked me to let Pipe know that she was headed to his room to help him. But Dad, you told me to always trust my gut. And something in his eyes didn't look right."

As soon as I was done explaining what had happened, Pipe took off like a bat out of hell with my dad, Irish, Coal, and Priest chasing after him.

Following them, every head in the clubhouse turned to watch what was going on.

And as long as I live, I will never forget that animalistic sound that reverberated throughout the clubhouse from Pipe.

**Gabby**

Something hard slammed into the right side of my face.

"Oww." I breathed out as I slowly came awake.

Closing my eyes and opening them again, I took in the area that I was in.

It looks like a dirty-looking warehouse with pallets of boxes and a few of them with big sheets over them.

"Why am I here?" I asked as I tried to take in a much-needed breath.

And when I heard a voice, I sneered. "We have a plan. I get you, and she gets Pipe, the fucking asshole piece of shit." Buster pointed to a woman that was standing with her arms crossed over her chest.

"You can go to hell. You'll never have me, and she will never have Pipe. Cause even if I left this world, he wouldn't be with another woman. So, you are both shit out of luck." I told them with as much venom and confidence I could muster.

Then Buster spoke in that nasal voice I can't stand and said, "Come on Gabby, don't be like that."

As soon as he brought his hand to what I guessed was to caress the side of my face, I turned my head and bit his hand, hard.

He yelped and jumped back.

And then my face whipped to the side when he smacked it again. He rounded me then and started to undo the ropes that were tying my hands while screaming, "I'm going to teach you a lesson, bitch. I was going to go nice and slow before, but not now, not fucking now. I'm going to ram my cock into your pussy, over and over again, and when that dries up, I'm going to ram it in your asshole."

He almost had my hands untied as I started running through what all I needed to do to get loose and get free.

"I'm not going to stand here and watch you fuck that whore. Call Pipe now and get his ass here." She screeched.

"I already know how to get your money, bitch. I don't need your help anymore." Buster told her as he pulled a gun out of the waistband of his jeans and pointed it at Rebecca, completely forgetting to remove the last rope around my wrists.

She opened her mouth to say something and then something rocked the warehouse when light streamed through the open doorway.

And there stood my man.

Arms at his sides, fist clenched, chest rising and falling rapidly.

The moment his eyes locked on mine and did a head-to-toe inspection, his eyes landed on my torn shirt and the cut on my face. It was not about to be a pretty scene.

I have never seen Pipe this mad, and I didn't want to ever have to see it again.

"Who put their hands on my daughter?" A man asked as he stepped out from behind Pipe while four men in suits took position on either side of him.

"Who the fuck are you?" Buster asked in a shrill tone.

"My name is Eduardo Costa."

That was my father's name. What the hell was happening here?

"Holy... fucking... shit," Buster mumbled.

"Ahh, I see you have heard of me. Now I'll ask one more time, who hit my daughter?"

But I didn't have my eyes on my father or on Buster. No, they were all on my man as he stepped further into the warehouse.

My body jolted when a shot rang out and suddenly Buster was screaming while holding his hand that no longer held a gun in his hand.

Snapping my head to the side, it was to see Coal lowering his own gun.

Pipe stepped closer to Rebecca and Buster, placing his body between them and me, and said in a tone I have never heard him use before, "You fucked up."

Craning my neck to see around him as Rebecca sneered and asked, "How?"

"You took the one thing that means the most to me in this world."

I watched as something crossed over her face, but it was gone in a split second. With venom lacing her words, she asked, "I never did, did I?"

"Nope. Because you never felt as though I was coming home. With Gabriella, I am home."

"How the fuck did y'all find us so fast?" Buster asked them.

"You dumped your phone, but guess you didn't tell my whore of an ex-wife that she needed to do the same."

"All the years I have given you and you speak to me like that?" Rebecca stuttered.

But it was Pipe's answer that had me wanting to climb him like a spider monkey.

"I told you, you fucked up Rebecca. Thought I loved you, but when I met Gabriella, I realized I never loved you. Because what I feel for her? Well, that trumps everything in my life, even my next breath. I would never talk to her like that, and if I did, you best believe I would shoot myself with my own gun."

"You good, honey?" Coal asked me and had my face not been on fire, I would have dropped my jaw to the floor.

I simply nodded and whispered, trying not to move my mouth too much, "I see what Adeline sees now. You got a sexy voice."

He laughed softly, shook his head, and then said something else to me, "Don't let Pipe hear you say that."

He grinned as I laughed and then winced when the movement made my face hurt all the more. "Gonna need stitches. You okay if I help you up?"

I nodded, and then, with Coal's help, stood on shaky legs.

I wasn't sure what had been in the syringe Buster had injected me with, but it was some strong stuff.

With Coal's arm wrapped around my waist, he helped me to the door and then stopped as we watched Pipe pull out his gun and shoot his ex-wife between the eyes.

Then he placed his gun back into his kutte and then walked over to a pipe that was on the floor, looked over to where we were standing, and said, "Darlin', need you out of this room for what I'm about to do."

"I'm not going anywhere until I'm in your arms and you're getting me out of this place. Besides, if you don't kill him, I'll have to do the job for you."

I heard, "That's my daughter." But I paid him no mind. He walked out on me. Never looked back.

With Coal's arm around my waist, I watched as Pipe took the lead pipe and broke every bone in Buster's body, and only then did he pull his gun out and shoot Buster right between the eyes.

He dropped the pipe as Whit, Charlie, and Irish grabbed fuel cans and started soaking the place in gasoline.

When he made it to me, I said, "You came for me."

"Always come for you, darlin', always." I smiled and then everything went black.

## Chapter 12
### Pipe

Seeing her eyes roll in the back of her head, that was something I never wanted to see again.

Hell, I didn't even think I could watch her do it when I bring her to climax again without remembering this moment.

And when I saw her about to drop to the floor, I dove for her. But I shouldn't have worried because Coal swept her up in his arms.

As my brothers set the warehouse on fire, I ran to the club truck and climbed in as Coal transferred my entire world to my arms.

Pagan climbed into the front seat of the truck and with the others climbing on their bikes, we raced to the hospital.

I hadn't worried about where her father and his men were.

Hell, I had been shocked as shit when he stepped out of his car at the clubhouse and only had to take one look at my face before he nodded, and simply said, *we will follow you.*

Just as that thought entered my head when we saw the hospital up ahead, the woman that meant everything to me started to seize in my arms.

I didn't have to say a word to Pagan as he swerved around the brothers and sped to the hospital, daring anyone to not move, or else they would get plowed the fuck over.

As soon as we entered the parking lot and raced to the entrance, I didn't even wait for the truck to come to a stop, opening the door and running full tilt into the emergency room. I ignored the metal detectors that were beeping behind me as a nurse raced over to me and asked what happened.

"She was drugged about an hour ago. She lost consciousness about fifteen minutes ago, and she started seizing about two minutes ago.

She nodded and said something and in a flurry of activity a gurney was wheeled over as a doctor and another nurse swarmed us as I laid Gabriella on the gurney, lowering my head I placed a kiss on her forehead and watched as they raced with her through the cream-colored painted doors.

The next two hours were a whirlwind as I gave them her information and then sat in a hard plastic chair with my brothers, her father and his men, and the women while we waited.

And as the doctor I had seen earlier stepped through the doors, I stood and said a silent prayer.

\*\*\*

Walking into Gabriella's room behind the doctor, the moment I saw her sitting in the bed I raced around the doctor and was at her side in a split second.

At her side, I placed my hand on the other side of her head and leaned in and inhaled her sweet scent, while whispering, "Hey, darlin'."

She chuckled softly and said, "Hey there, honey."

She brought her finger to her lips and tapped it, telling me what she wanted.

Grinning, I accommodated her and brought my mouth to hers, not giving a damn that the doctor wanted to tell us both what was going on since she was awake and alert.

"Hi, Mrs. Childers, I doubt you remember my name, but I am Doctor Amallo. When we did the tox screen, we saw that you had a dose of chloroform in your system. Now normally once it's run its course, usually there are no lasting side effects. However, that isn't the case for women in your condition."

Gabriella scrunched her brows when she asked, "Condition? What do you mean?"

"Well, did you know you were pregnant?" He asked her, then looked at me.

And together we both shook our heads and I said, "She has an IUD."

He nodded. "A certain number of things can cause the IUD to dislodge." He cleared his throat and suddenly I knew what he meant.

Gabriella looked at me and busted out laughing. "You are big, honey."

I shrugged at her with pride filling every pore in my body, but then I remembered, "Is she still? Pregnant, I mean? The drug wouldn't have caused her to lose it, right?"

"We are waiting for OB to get here and perform a scan to check. Also, to see how far along you are." He nodded at us and then there was a knock on the door as a woman in pink scrubs walked in pushing a machine.

And there on that monitor after everything was ready, and yes, I growled at the doctor when he stood where he was as the tech inserted the probe up my wife's vagina.

The good doctor moved so he could still see the screen and not my wife's vagina.

There on the monitor, we saw a little blob that confirmed we were indeed pregnant.

Looking down at my wife, I asked, "Happy?"

She didn't bother to take her eyes from the screen, knowing I wanted her eyes instead of staring at our baby. I found that I hadn't minded it in the slightest, not even when she whispered, "Ecstatic. Are you?"

"Fifth best day of my life," I told her as I pressed a kiss to her forehead.

The day's events played on a loop while we waited for them to discharge her. But it wouldn't be for a few hours, so everyone had headed home.

Gabriella had also found out why her father had distanced himself from her all those years ago. The reason he had no contact with her until now is that he was starting his empire and he didn't want anyone to know about her and use her to hurt him.

And yes, her father was the head of a Mexican cartel.

Shaking my head that my wife was the daughter of a cartel boss I looked at my woman who had a gleam in her eyes, and before I could ask her what that was about, she said tiredly, "You have some master swimmers there, honey. Only been sleeping together for four weeks, means you had to have knocked me up the first time we had sex."

"Just means this baby was meant to be. How long have you been wanting to say that to me?"

"Since he told us we were pregnant." I chuckled at her and then settled my body around hers on the bed. And yes, half of my body was hanging off it. They needed bigger ones.

\*\*\*

My woman was starting to waddle. We were six months pregnant and just found out that we were having a baby boy.

And for some reason, driving over an hour to a certain store when I was dog tired didn't bother me. Not in the least. Not like it had before with my ex-wife.

I was really driving over an hour away because there was one store that carried the kind of fudge that Gabriella liked.

But I knew like I knew the back of my hand, and even if she wasn't carrying my baby, I would be driving to get this fudge, anyway.

My phone rang just as I was checking out at the store. Pulling it out of my pocket, I checked the display, seeing my woman in her wedding dress, and answered immediately, "Hey, darlin'."

"Where are you?" The hurried expression had my spine straightening.

"About to leave the store. Are you okay?" And the answer that followed that, well, I wanted to laugh my ass off.

"Yeah, now I want a cheeseburger and onion rings. Please?" She asked and I knew she was poking out her bottom lip.

Grinning, I nodded, checked the total, and handed the cashier a twenty-dollar bill. However, she hadn't seen it because she was eyeing me up and down, and I didn't like it one bit.

Snapping, I said, "Hey, quit eye fucking me and take the money."

I shouldn't have said that. Oh, hell no, I shouldn't have. Because I heard, "Hand that bitch the fucking phone."

"No, I will not hand the phone to her," I said into the phone, then I said to the cashier, "Take my money so I can go get home to my wife. My very pregnant wife wants this fudge and a cheeseburger and onion rings. One that will not hesitate to come down here and kick your ass."

"Has she taken your money yet?" She asked me shrilly, huffing, just as the cashier ducked her head and took my money.

"She just did," I told her and had to smile. "You were putting your shoes on, weren't you?"

"You bet your ass I was. You're mine. They can stare all they want because I take it as a compliment but eye fucking you? Over my dead body." And when everyone around me started staring open-mouthed at me, I raised my brow and then it hit me, my cheek had hit the speaker button.

"Whoops," I said as I tapped the speaker button.

"Why are you saying whoops?" Gabriella asked as I took the change, grabbed my bag, and walked out of the store and to my bike.

"My cheek hit the speaker button."

I could practically hear her nod as laughter followed. Shaking my head, I told her I loved her and then hung up the phone.

I barely made it in the door when I heard, "Gimmie. Gimmie. Gimmie." She called out as she raced down the hall to meet me in nothing but my t-shirt and those knee-high socks she loves so much.

Snorting, I handed the bags over to her, and when she opened one and inhaled, I swear she made a sound that I didn't even hear in the bedroom.

And before she turned to the bedroom to devour the contents, she stepped closer to me, got on her tiptoes, and puckered her lips.

Kissing her back, I laughed as she all but spun a one-eighty and headed straight to our bedroom.

That gorgeous ass was swaying even though she was waddling.

At first, I had felt terrible about getting her pregnant.

Only because of how tiny she is and how big I am.

So, there I lay with my head on my woman's belly, talking softly to my baby while my woman chowed down on all of the goodies I had brought her.

Normally, I would have asked for a piece of fudge, but I learned in the early stages of this pregnancy never to take food from a pregnant woman.

Because she was going to flip the killer psycho switch that lived in all pregnant women.

Which was why not even a few minutes later there was a piece of the decadent fudge in my face.

Smiling, I grabbed it, pressed a kiss on her belly which told her thanks, and ate my piece of fudge.

***

"Honey, I can see it on your face. It's practically green." I told her as another smell of fish wafted towards us. Even at thirty-eight weeks, my woman still couldn't handle the smell of fish. She fucking hated it.

However, she hadn't gotten ill when we had that Cajun boil a few weeks ago at the clubhouse, so I had thought that this place would be okay. It obviously wasn't.

"You want to eat here, Caiden. You've had enough of not being able to do what you want to do. I won't stand for it anymore." She said as she spoke with her nose pinched closed.

I shook my head then, "Even at the expense of you puking your guts up. I'm one lucky motherfucker."

Then I looked at the hostess, and said, "The smells are making her sick. Please cancel our reservation."

"Caiden!" She exclaimed as I did that, not giving a damn how it sounded to them.

Turning so my chest was pressed to hers, I bent slightly so I didn't put any pressure on her protruding belly. Then I placed my hand on the side of her neck, lowered my head, and said, "You are the light of my life, darlin'. I'll always put you first. Our children second, and the club third. I don't care that I've been wanting to eat here. I care about you."

Tears immediately welled in her eyes as she muttered, "Freaking hormones."

I couldn't help the chuckle that slipped out as I wiped a tear that escaped and ran down her cheek while saying, "Come on gorgeous, let's go eat at that place over on Fourth Street."

"We ate there last week." She told me. I knew she felt bad, but she didn't need to. I enjoyed hearing her moan more than I did the food, and that was A-okay in my book.

After we ate, we went by the clubhouse to see what was going on, where we stayed for an hour and then headed home.

We had just laid down when I felt my woman tense.

And then I felt it, the wetness around my knees.

"What the fuck?" I asked into the darkened room.

"I think… I think my water just broke."

And yes, even though we had gone over this a hundred times, no joke, what we needed to do so we could head to the hospital, I still froze.

But it was my woman's wail of pain that had me snapping into focus, grabbing our bags, and hauling ass out to my truck.

Running back into the house, I helped Gabriella out to the truck, not even caring I was in a pair of sweats I had grabbed off the floor that she hated seeing me wear in public and a t-shirt with my kutte on.

"If any of the nurses stare at your junk in those, I am burning them." She snapped as I helped her with her seat belt.

I would've laughed at her possessive nature, but I was too busy freaking out.

I was in the truck and headed to the clubhouse when she told me she sent a text to Stella knowing that she would spread the word that we were about to be having a baby.

***

If I ever thought that another woman was weak, I wanted to be slapped upside the head.

Because in the throes of labor as the nurses and doctors raced around the room, Gabriella almost broke my hand with how hard she was squeezing it, trying to get through her contractions.

I almost begged her to get the epidural but with one look from her face I kept my mouth fucking shut.

Then when I heard the terrible wail coming from my woman because of the pain she had to be in, I made a vow then and there that I would only be going through this once.

I couldn't handle seeing her in this kind of pain.

But whatever vow I made; my woman obliterated that shit with a smile on her face.

Because not only after eight hours of labor did we welcome our son, Thayne Caiden Childers, into the world, but exactly ten months later, whoops, we welcomed our daughter, Madeline Alora Childers, into the world.

Fuck the vow I made to her.

But that would be the only one I would ever break.

As I sit here in our little girl's nursery, rocking her back to sleep so my woman could get some sleep because she had her final exam and she would have an associate degree in business, I thanked God for having Rebecca in my life.

Had I not realized how horrible she was, I never would've opened my eyes and noticed the most perfect angel to ever walk this earth was right there within arm's reach.

Just then my little boy walked into the nursery, climbed up my sweatpants-covered leg, and settled in my other arm.

I hadn't heard the click of my woman's camera that night, because I had fallen asleep with the two other humans that held my heart in their hands.

I only noticed that she had clicked the button on her camera a week later, because there beside the pictures Stella took of us the day I made Gabriella my ole' lady was that picture of the three of us, crammed into a white rocking chair, with all our mouths open as we slept.

# Epilogue
## Pipe

Pulling my bike into our garage, I shut her down, then stretched my aching back. I was fifty-one years old and being on the back of my bike for eight hours straight, only stopping to top off the tank did something to my back.

It felt great to stretch even when it was hurting like a motherfucker.

Getting off my bike, I removed my helmet and walked it over to the wall, and hung it on the peg right beside Gabriella's, Thayne's, and Madeline's.

Walking in our mud room, I toed off my boots and then something delicious from the kitchen filled my senses. And I didn't miss the lights she left on, knowing I appreciated it.

As soon as I rounded the corner, I noticed a plate with foil covering it sitting on the island along with a note, two Advil, and a bottle of water. These were the small things I had always wondered about, how they would feel. And still, sixteen years later, my woman never failed to do stuff like this for me.

Snatching up the note, I read it and couldn't contain the smile that formed on my face. *'Honey, I know your back has to be hurting, take the pills, and drink the water. The plate has those cream cheese brownies you love so much on it. You can eat one before your dinner, which has been keeping warm in the oven, then you can eat as many brownies as you want. Then come to bed. You know I don't sleep right when you're not next to me. Your wife.'*

Grinning, I removed the foil and took a small brownie, and popped it in my mouth, then after I took the medicine and drank the water, I took the plate out of the oven, and grinned.

Country fried steak, mashed potatoes with gravy, and green beans. Goddamn, my woman could cook was the only thought that entered my head as the flavors burst over my tongue.

After I ate, I loaded the plate and fork in the dishwasher, grabbed two brownies, killed the lights, and ate both of them on my way to the bedroom.

Seeing my woman curled up on my side of the bed did something to my heart.

Even all these years later, my woman never ceased to amaze me.

Walking to her, I bent my head and placed a gentle kiss on her forehead which had her mumbling tiredly, "I love you."

"I love you too, darlin'," I told her as I started to strip and tossed my clothes in the hamper in the bathroom.

Allowing the hot water to run over me, I washed my hair and my body, then shut the water off.

And yeah, I did it again, forgot to grab a fucking towel.

Shaking my head at my own stupidity, I opened the shower door and saw a towel hanging there for me.

I didn't even have to ask or hesitate as I grabbed it and wrapped the warm fluffy white towel around my body and dried off.

The moment I had my woman in my arms, I curled my body around hers and felt her entire body heft out a sigh as she pressed her body into mine and promptly fell right to sleep.

And yes, I thanked God every single day for this woman in my life.

Most men had something close to this, but they didn't have what I did with my woman.

And that right there made me the luckiest son of a bitch alive.

### Gabby

"I want this." I looked up from my book when I heard Madeline say that.

"What do you want, sweetheart?" I asked her as I looked at the mantle above the fireplace and saw the picture she was looking at.

"I want a man to look at me like Dad does at you in this picture." She was talking about one of the pictures that was my favorite.

The memory of that day flooded my mind, and I recalled how it felt to have his arm around me as I led him to the exact spot where that truck had been parked and we had chilled in the water with that blue tarp keeping everything in.

I had turned in Pipe's arms and had my Property of Pipe kutte visible and he was looking down at me with love and pride in his eyes. Stella had captured that shot perfectly.

The others were awesome, but they weren't my favorite.

"You will, one day when you're ready. And when that happens, I hope you realize it for what it is and hold on to it with both hands, sweetheart."

"What are we talking about?" I looked over at my man and my son as they walked into the house.

Even with gray around his temples, he was still the most handsome thing I had ever seen.

And when Madeline told him what she told me, I watched as his protective side came out and he said in a growl, "No. Nope. No. You will wait until you're at least thirty before that happens, and he better understand that he has to go through me first."

And my son, being my man's clone, said, "Add me to the list. You're my little sister, and they also gotta go through me first."

Oh, but something later in the day had me thinking that it had already happened because apparently everyone else had missed the way a certain brother had looked at our girl.

But sure enough, I hadn't missed it, not by a long shot.

Standing there in the back part of the clubhouse, I smiled at all the little kids that were running around, remembering how I had gotten here sixteen years ago.

Things had sure changed in all those years, but one thing hadn't. And that was how the club girls would go after the men and didn't care if they were taken or not.

And as I stood there and watched one in particular sidle up to my man, I didn't even move from my spot.

Because as soon as she reached a hand out to touch him, he stepped back and then pointed to where I was standing, and started my way.

I watched as the girl pouted, which had me laughing softly, and then she started to follow him but was stopped by my daughter who said, rather loudly, "That's my dad, whore. My dad, who happens to love my mother with everything in him. So much so that he even offered to get her name tattooed on his forehead so bitches like you would know to leave him the fuck alone. Now, this is the second time you've been warned. You try it again and nobody will hold my mother back from beating the dog shit out of you. And trust me, you don't want that, just ask Cortney over there when she tried to sit in his lap when I was nine years old. And in case you missed it, my mother used to be a club girl, too. Let that settle in." I watched as my girl had my back and when Carmella heard I used to be a club girl too, she nodded and backed away.

That night I lay in our bed while our kids stayed at the clubhouse to have a *Top Gun* marathon in the new media room Asher had built. Knowing they were safe, I curled my body further into my husband's and smiled.

Because when I did that, he muttered in his sleep, "Love you, darlin'."

And then my husband started sawing logs with his snoring.

Laughing softly, I closed my eyes and thanked my lucky stars for the life I have.

My kids had a family that, in case anything ever happened to us, they would be taken care of.

I had a thriving online business doing embroidery work and sewing, which I loved.

We also had the help of the Mexican cartel should we ever need it, thanks to my father, who had spent the last sixteen years making up the time that was lost with me and our kids.

Oh, and the promise that Pipe had offered to make right? He did that when he called my father while we were on our honeymoon.

The other one with my mother? Well, he left her alone. He only had Charlie hack into her and her husband's accounts and send their money to charity. The rightful charity where they said their money was going, but wasn't. They were arrested on embezzlement charges, and I can neither confirm nor deny if my father played a hand in the two of them being shanked in the yard and bleeding out.

Moral of the story, karma is a bitch. It can either kick your ass seven ways to Sunday or it can reward you with the greatest treasures of life.

Like me.

And this was the story of how a club girl got her happily ever after with a man she never saw coming.

One who loved her unconditionally.

And one that, with the help from her, let down those walls around his heart and allowed her to slip on in while she turned his heart from a block of ice into something to be revered.

The End.

## Thank You Note

I wanted to thank you for taking the time out of your day to read Pipe and Gabriella's story.

If you are going through something, I hope it helped you.

If you needed a reminder that you are badass and awesome, I hope this helped you.

So, if you are wondering when Zagan MC comes out, it will be the end of 2023. I have a few more books that need to happen before I introduce an all-new MC to you guys. The plan is for one series, and one chapter with Zagan MC, in Mississippi, but who knows.

As always, thank you soooo much for reading Cold As Ice.

Y'all are the reason I do what I do.

As always,

Xoxo Tiffany Casper.

# Other Works

## Wrath MC

**Mountain of Clearwater**

Clearwater's Savior

Clearwater's Hope

Clearwater's Fire

Clearwater's Miracle

Clearwater's Treasure

Clearwater's Luck

Clearwater's Redemption

Christmas in Clearwater

**Dogwood's Treasures**

Dove's Life

Phoenix's Plight

Raven's Climb

Wren's Salvation

Lo's Wraith

Falcon's Rise

Sparrow's Grace (July 2022)

Lark's Precious (September 2022)

## DeLuca Empire

The Devil & The Siren

The Cleaner & The Princess

The Soldier & The Dancer (September 2022)

The Shadow & The Mafia Princess (November 2022)

## Willow Creek

Where Hearts Align

Where Hearts Connect (August 2022)

Where Hearts Grow (October 2022)

Where Hearts Mend (November 2022)

## Pinewood Lake

Book 1 (January 2023)

Book 2 (February 2023)

Book 3 (March 2023)

## As If...

Cold As Ice

Dark As Coal (August 2022)

Smooth As Whiskey (October 2022)

**Novella's**

Hotter Than Sin

Silver Treasure

Wrath Ink

## Connect With Me

### My Website
https://tiffanycasper.com

### Facebook
https://www.facebook.com/author.tiffany.casper

### Instagram
https://www.instagram.com/authortiffanycasper/

### Goodreads
https://www.goodreads.com/author/show/19027352.Tiffany_Casper

Made in the USA
Middletown, DE
18 February 2025